A Fair of the Heart

WELCOME TO REDEMPTION, BOOK 1

DONNA MARIE ROGERS

ISBN: 978-1-941829-07-3
Published by Donna Kowalczyk
Contact Information: www.DonnaMarieRogers.com

Cover Design: The Killion Group, Inc.
Interior Formatting: Author E.M.S.

Published in the United States of America.

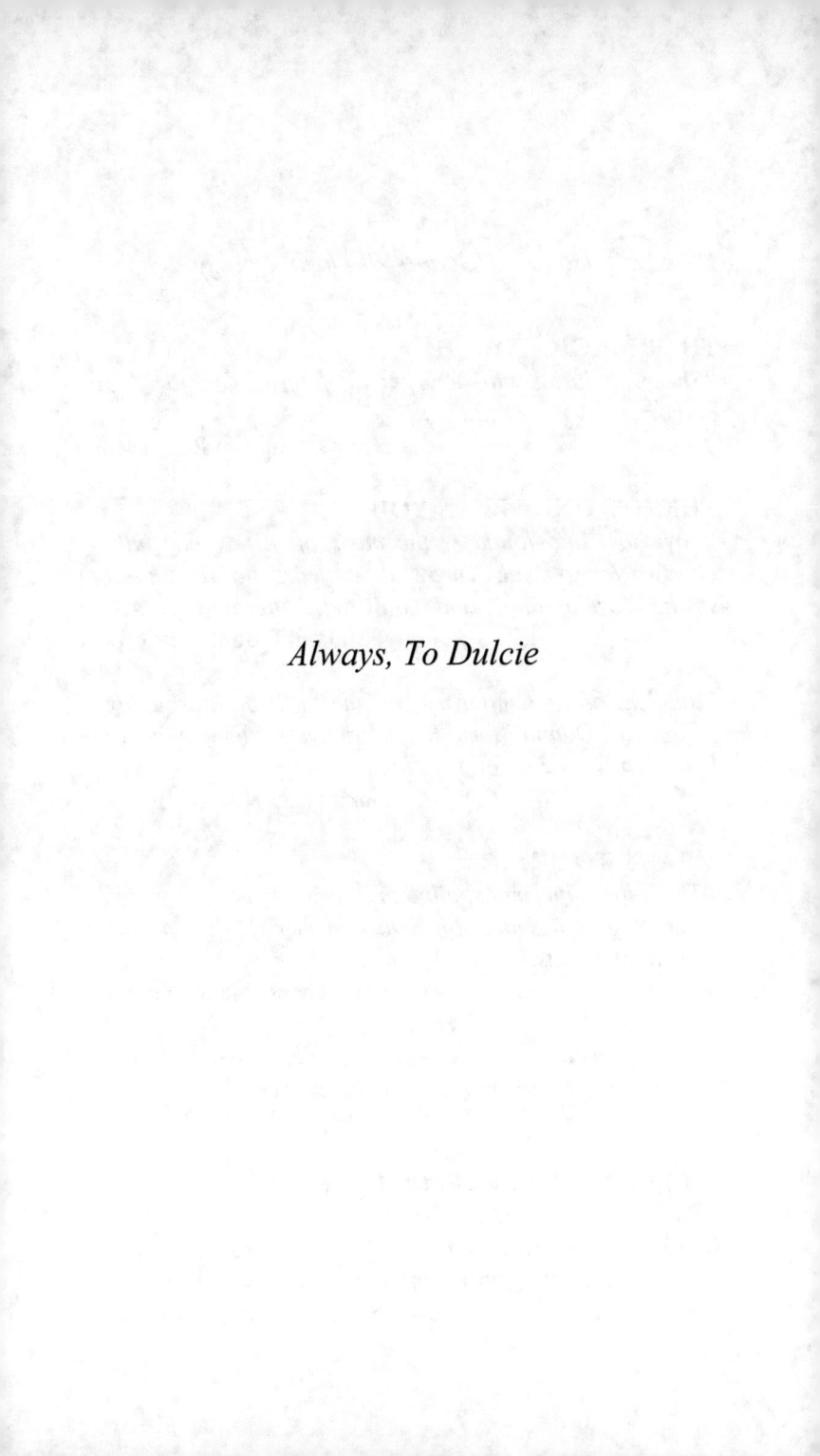

Always, To Dulcie

Praise for Donna Marie Rogers

THAT MAGIC TOUCH
"Sheer genius. I will now put all future books by this author on my must read list."
—5 Stars, Amazon Reviewer

THERE'S ONLY BEEN YOU
"Love lost and found is the basis of this wonderfully heartwarming read. Throw in a years-old lie and a strong sense of family and it only gets better and better."
—4 Stars, RT Book Reviews

"Readers of contemporary romance will be thoroughly delighted...Donna Marie Rogers delivers a tender tale of love, family, and second chances."
—5 Bookmarks, Wild on Books

MEANT TO BE
"The plot kept me spellbound throughout the entire book. Rogers has the ability to keep her readers on the edge of our seats."
—5 Hearts, The Romance Studio

"The material is tightly written, well plotted and fast paced, and the characters are unforgettable."
—5 Books, Long and Short Reviews

WELCOME TO REDEMPTION SERIES
"With their easy, breezy style and skilled characterizations, Rogers and Netzel have created a town that readers won't want to leave."
—4½ Stars – RT Book Reviews

Donna Marie Rogers' Titles

LAKE SHELBYVILLE SERIES
That Magic Touch

JAMISON FAMILY SERIES
There's Only Been You
Foolish Pride
Meant To Be

DOUBLE M RANCH SERIES
Golden Opportunity
Golden Dream

WELCOME TO REDEMPTION SERIES
(small town romance series with Stacey Joy Netzel)
A Fair of the Heart (Book 1)
The Perfect Blend (Book 3)
Home Is Where the Heart Is (Book 5)
Never Let Me Go (Book 7)
Say You Love Me (Book 9)

Chapter One

"*I* believe this is yours."

Lauren Frazier met the teasing gaze of the handsome stranger standing on her porch as he handed over the knob to her front door. She promptly burst out laughing, examining the ancient piece of crap with a shake of her head.

"Sorry," she said, bringing it down to a chuckle. "But the handle on my back door fell off earlier this morning."

The stranger grinned. "I might stay home today, if I were you."

"Ya think?" She tossed the knob on the floor beside the shoe rack and stepped back. "So, what can I do for you?"

His keen brown eyes searched her living room and then the kitchen, his confusion obvious. "I'm not sure if I'm in the right place…do you cut hair?"

"I do. Sorry, the beauty shop sign fell off the house a few weeks ago."

His lips twitched. "I need a trim. The librarian recommended you. Said you work out of your home." He held out his hand. "Caleb Hunter."

"I'll have to send Matt a thank-you note. Lauren Frazier." She shook his hand, and then gestured him inside. "I work out of my mud room. It's just off the kitchen."

He followed her through the house into the mudroom, which doubled as both her laundry room and her single-chair hair salon.

After a quick glance around, he sat down in the barber chair and leaned back with his long legs sprawled out. "Don't think I've ever seen one of these in someone's house before."

"I got a deal on it from a salon in Green Bay that closed last year." Lauren studied him from the corner of her eye as she pulled out a clean plastic cape and her trimming shears. Roughly six feet tall, with broad shoulders, slim hips, and a muscular upper body, Mr. Caleb Hunter could have walked right off the cover of GQ magazine. He had big, bedroom brown eyes, full sexy lips, and a patrician nose that looked as if it'd seen a fist or two. His crowning glory, a thick mop of wavy auburn hair, needed at least an inch trimmed off—Lauren itched to run her fingers through it.

Thank you, Matt.

She stepped up behind him and covered him with the cape, securing it with a hair clip. His heady masculine scent assailed her senses, and Lauren resisted the urge to lean in and get a big whiff of his spicy aftershave. Whoa, girl, get a grip. He met her gaze in the mirror, and she swore she saw blatant interest in his eyes. She ran a comb through his hair. "You've got a gorgeous head of hair, Caleb Hunter. So, who's to thank, your mom or dad?"

He cleared his throat, and if Lauren didn't know any better, she'd swear her innocent little question had upset him.

"Sorry, didn't mean to pry. It's part of the job, you know? Make small talk."

"I know. It's just...I lost my mother recently."

Lauren's hands froze. "I'm so sorry. Open mouth, insert foot. That's me."

"You couldn't have known. Don't worry about it."

DONNA MARIE ROGERS

Lauren nodded and got back to work on his hair. She'd love to ask him a few more questions, like what's his sign, boxers or briefs, top or bottom, but thought better of it. Good God, the man's mother just died. Not to mention, the last thing she wanted or needed was a man in her life—although if Bob Vila showed up on her doorstep right about now, she'd drop down on bended knee so fast it'd make his head spin.

She met Caleb's gaze in the mirror again. "So, are you planning to go to the fair this weekend?"

"I hadn't thought about it," he admitted. "Guess I might take a walk through."

After brushing the hair clippings from his neck and shoulders, Lauren swept the cape away and tried to hand him a mirror.

He waved it away and pulled out his wallet. "I'm sure it's fine. So what do I owe you?"

"Ten bucks." She accepted the twenty he handed her and opened her cashbox to pull out a ten.

"Keep it," he said. "Put it toward a new doorknob."

With a grateful nod, she stuck the bill back in the box. "Thanks."

Caleb winked at her and turned to leave. He stepped on a loose floorboard on his way to the door. "Your husband's not much of a handyman, is he?"

"I'm divorced. And, no, he never was much of a handyman. Philandering? Now, there's a sport he excelled at."

"I'm sorry. I didn't mean—"

She waved him off. "Consider us even in the foot-in-mouth department."

He held her gaze for a moment, and then casually glanced around. Lauren inwardly cringed. By the time her ex had left her for greener pastures of the big-boobed variety, the house had pretty much been falling down around her ears. And with only one income to pay the bills, mortgage, and take care of her two kids, there wasn't much leftover for home repairs.

"I'm not very handy either, as you can see." She shrugged, making no apologies for her lack of carpentry skills.

He surprised her with a soft chuckle. "Yep. Got that. Listen, I have some free time later this afternoon. It wouldn't take me long to do some general repairs."

Lauren stared at him for several heartbeats, at a loss for words. No one had ever offered to help before. "I appreciate it, but...well, truth is I wouldn't be able to pay you much. And by much, I mean nothing." She gave him a cheeky grin.

"I wouldn't accept your money anyway. I was thinking more along the lines of old-fashioned bartering."

She crossed her arms and cocked a brow. "You're entering dangerous territory, Mr. Hunter." Okay, so the guy was a hottie. Didn't mean she'd jump into bed with him to get a few doorknobs reattached or a few loose boards nailed down. Or the closet door in Emma's room put back on track, or the screen in Max's bedroom window patched, or replacing the vanity door hinges in the upstairs bathroom, or—

"I meant supper, Ms. Frazier. As in a home-cooked meal? Haven't had one in years and thought a couple hours of home repairs might be worth some meatloaf and mashed potatoes, maybe some buttered rolls."

Lauren's cheeks grew hot, surprising her. Blushing? Her? Now there's a novelty. "I can do supper. Although my son, Max, might run away from home if I made meatloaf. How about chicken and rice bake, and some of those pop-open crescent rolls?"

"Throw in dessert, and it's a deal."

Lauren leaned a hip against the wall. "Well, now, dessert is a whole other ballgame. Especially 'home-cooked' dessert."

He grinned. "Name your price."

"Max's bottom dresser drawer. It's been stuck shut for months."

"Chocolate?"

"What else?"

He stuck out his hand. "Deal."

Caleb stopped at the library on his way back to Lauren's house to recheck-out the Electrician's Handbook. Matt Jacobs looked up when he entered, a grin replacing his studious frown.

"Finally got that mop trimmed, I see. So, did you end up going to Lauren or old man Krause?"

Caleb set the book on the counter and browsed through the stack waiting to be put back on the shelves. "I got called into the barbershop to fix some shelving yesterday. Old man Krause's hand was shaking so hard, it's a miracle he didn't clip his customer's ear off. I went to Lauren's."

Matt laughed. He walked over and picked up the handbook. "What do you think? Ready for the exam?"

"Ready as I'll ever be. I'd like to check it back out, though, read it one last time before I take the exam. Probably next Friday."

"Thinking about staying in Redemption then?"

Caleb swiped his hand through his newly shorn hair. After returning to the states from active duty, he hadn't felt...comfortable returning to his hometown. He'd ended up heading to Chicago with a fellow army buddy, where he'd spent the last thirteen years doing carpentry work, plumbing, and even dabbling in electricity. He'd discovered a talent for the latter, and after several months of studying, finally felt ready to take the licensing exam.

But stay in Redemption permanently? Truth be told, he was torn. He'd only meant to stay for a few days, but upon returning home for his mother's funeral, Caleb had felt the strongest sense of peace. Usually, he couldn't wait to get the hell outta Dodge.

He'd talked to his boss just the night before, and the gruff old codger had made it clear—Caleb had one week to return, or he wouldn't have a job waiting for him when he did. And yet, despite the warning, Caleb took on two more jobs just that morning, extending his stay in Redemption indefinitely.

It wasn't as if he had anyone special waiting for him back in Chicago anyway. Caleb had dated plenty of women over the years, but he'd never been the relationship type. Not that he couldn't be faithful to one woman. He'd just never met one that held his interest long enough, or that he'd wanted to get to know on a deeper level.

Until today.

"It's a definite possibility." Caleb tossed his keys and caught them with a jingle. "Catch you later, Matt."

He arrived at Lauren's house around three-thirty. She stood on the front porch waving a brand new doorknob assembly, still in the package, and sporting a huge grin. A white tank top and stonewashed low rider Levis showed off a great tan and incredible body. Her shoulder-length, honey blond curls were held up on either side of her beautiful face by gold barrettes, and small hoops hung from her earlobes. Eyes as blue as Lake Michigan twinkled up at him.

"Love the tool belt," she said, gesturing him inside.

"I have backup in my car. Electric drill, power saw, grenades."

"Funny."

He stepped inside and sniffed the air. "Wow, if chicken bake tastes as good as it smells, I may start breaking your furniture myself."

"No need. I make it at least once a week. Both my kids love it."

At that moment, an adorable little pipsqueak dashed in from the kitchen, blond curls bobbing all around. She wrapped her arms around Lauren's legs and gazed up at him with wide-eyed curiosity. She was the spitting image of her mother, complete with a perfect Cupid's bow mouth, flawless alabaster skin, and those same gorgeous blue eyes. In twenty years, she'd also have Lauren's incredible figure—slim and sleek, yet curved in all the right places.

Caleb crouched down and winked at her. She couldn't have been more than three years old. "Hey, punkin, my name's Caleb. What's yours?"

"Em-ma." She glanced up at her mother. "I not puck'in."

Lauren ruffled her daughter's curls. "It just means cutie pie. Like what I call you."

"Oh." She turned back to Caleb and squinted thoughtfully. "Momma make choc'it cake. I helped."

Caleb's heart swelled in his chest. He had to clear his throat to speak. "And I bet it's the yummiest chocolate cake ever."

Emma gave a solemn nod, and then skipped off into the kitchen.

Caleb stood back up and met Lauren's gaze. "Well? What should I tackle first?"

She held up the new doorknob package. "Being able to lock my doors at night is my number one priority. And thank you. Again."

Caleb felt as if he were drowning in those big baby blues. "My pleasure. You did, after all, make 'choc'it' cake."

Lauren grinned. "From scratch, too."

"Well, then, guess I'd better go earn my supper."

By the time he'd put the new knob on the front door and reattached the handle to the back screen door, supper was just about ready. He decided a stuck drawer would take all of five minutes, and had Lauren direct him to Max's room.

Typical boy's room, he thought as he glanced around. Basketball hoop hanging on the back of the door, unmade bed, sports paraphernalia everywhere. The kid was a huge Green Bay Packers fan: Packer curtains, Packer bedspread, Packer wallpaper border. The room was neater than Caleb would've expected, too—not so much as a dirty sock on the floor. No doubt Lauren's doing.

Caleb located the dresser in question and knelt down to try the drawer. Yep, stuck shut.

Once he pried it open, he'd plane it down a bit, which should do the trick. He worked the drawer back and forth, surprised when a couple of folded-up playing cards fell out. Hmm. And the drawer seemed to open and close fine now. A flash of red caught his eye. An all-too-familiar flash of red. Caleb exhaled a hard breath as he pulled out a flip-top box of cigarettes.

"Whad'ya think you're doing?"

Caleb's head snapped up. Standing in the doorway, hands fisted at his sides, was a blue-eyed boy who could only be Max. He looked to be about twelve or thirteen, with much darker hair than his mother's, but just as curly. And he wore a scowl the size of Texas. "Fixing your stuck drawer." He climbed to his feet and held up the cigarette box. "You do realize these things'll stunt your growth, right?"

The kid's eyes grew suspiciously red, but his expression remained mutinous. "You had no right going through my stuff!"

"Maybe not, but lucky for you I did. You're too young to smoke, son, and—"

"Who the hell are you, and why are you even in my room?" the kid demanded.

The quick beat of feet on the stairs reached Caleb a second before Lauren burst into the

12

room. "What in the world is going on up here? Max, what's the problem?"

Caleb tucked the cigarette box in his back pocket while Lauren's attention was on her son. Later, when they were alone, he'd show them to her. Caleb knew the kid was going through a rough time, and while he hated to be the bearer of bad news, Lauren needed to know so she could nip the problem in the bud.

"Nothin'," Max snapped.

"Your son wasn't too happy to find a stranger in his room, and he told me so. He thought I was snooping through his stuff."

Max met Caleb's gaze, some of his hostility dissipating. Not much, but some.

Lauren eyed them both with suspicion. "Supper's on the table. Max, go wash your hands, please."

Max stormed from the room, and a few seconds later a door slammed.

Lauren flinched. "I'm sorry. Ever since his father left, he's been...different. He blames me. He's too young to understand what really happened, and I guess it's easier to make me the bad guy since I'm still here. Ten-year-old mentality," she finished with a shrug.

"Ten? Wow, big kid."

"Big father."

Caleb wished there was something he could do or say to ease her burden. And Max's troubles were worse than she knew if the kid was smoking. "He'll settle down, don't worry. And I'll help any way I can."

Christ, what the hell was he thinking, offering to get involved in their family problems? He barely knew the woman. Though if he were being honest with himself, he wanted to get to know her better. Much better.

The thought scared the living tar out of him, but didn't stop him from taking a step forward.

Chapter Two

Lauren could only stare at this incredible man who'd done more for her in a couple of hours than anyone else had in years. Could he possibly be for real? She'd spent nearly ten years with a man who'd made her feel worthless and sexless, sleeping with any willing warm body he could find. Lauren desperately wanted to believe her time had come, that her numbers had been drawn and she was the grand prize winner. What a pleasure it would be to finally have someone to lean on, to help shoulder the burden her life had become. To love her and only her.

Wow. Where in the world had that come from?

They gazed at each other for several heartbeats before she said, "That's a mighty generous offer considering you barely know us."

Caleb took another step toward her. "I was hoping we could rectify that."

"I..." Lauren mentally chastised herself. What was it about this man that made coherent speech a thing of the past? Or her heart pitter-patter like a teenage girl in the throes of puppy love? Freakin' embarrassing is what it was.

Caleb propped his hands on his hips. "I didn't mean to make you uncomfortable. It's just...either I'm way off my game or there's a spark between us."

Lauren tucked a curl behind her ear, and then huffed another out of her face. She met his gaze and became lost again in those incredible bedroom brown eyes. All he had to do was look at a woman, and she'd follow him straight into the bedroom. The Pied Piper of Redemption. Lauren swallowed down a giggle. "You're not."

"Pardon?"

"Off your game. You're not. But Caleb—"

"Come on, now, no 'but'. We haven't even had a meal together yet, and already with the 'but'."

He grinned, and Lauren forgot the rest of what she'd planned to say. He was right. Probably be a good idea to see if he chewed with his mouth open before making a final decision on 'but'. "Well then, get ready for the best chicken bake in all the land. Complete with green bean casserole, creamy cucumbers, and plenty of crescent rolls."

He clapped his hands together and gave them a gleeful rub. "Lead the way, beautiful lady, 'cause I'm hungry as a bear."

Beautiful lady. Wow. Let's see, he can fix most anything, he appreciates a home-cooked meal, Emma hasn't stopped chattering about him, and he wins the award for best view in all of Redemption. Oh yeah, this one definitely has promise.

She led the way downstairs, knocking on the bathroom door as they passed by. "Come on, Max, time to eat."

Lauren tried not to worry when Max didn't come down for supper. If he wanted to sulk in his room all night, fine. Frankly, she was tired of his piss-poor attitude and snarky comments. It was nice, for a change, eating a meal without insults being hurled at her between bites.

And it was such a joy watching Caleb flirt with Emma, and watching Emma flirt right back. She was her mother's daughter for sure. Although, she was doing a much better job with Caleb than Lauren. No nervous stutters or sweaty palms for Emma. And if Lauren didn't know better, she'd swear Caleb was falling just as hard for little Miss Poopy Pants.

By the time Lauren sliced into the chocolate cake, her trouble detector had hit high alert. Max was a big kid for his age, with double the appetite of a normal ten-year-old, and chicken bake was his favorite meal. But if that wasn't reason enough to worry, Max should've raced down the stairs the moment that cake dome was lifted.

After serving Caleb a hunk of cake, and Emma a sliver, Lauren rose to her feet and excused herself. The bathroom door was now open and the light on, so she stuck her head inside. Empty. She checked his bedroom—also empty—then her own room in case he'd decided to play computer games. No Max. She ran back downstairs and checked the spare room in the back of the house where he played video games. Full-blown panic set in when she discovered that room empty as well.

Tears stung her eyes. She dabbed at them with her fingers and composed herself before returning to the kitchen.

Caleb looked up and his smile faded. "What is it?"

She guessed she hadn't done such a great job on the composing part. "I can't find Max. He's not in the house, and since we would've heard him if he'd left through the front door, he must've snuck out a window."

Caleb shot to his feet and closed the distance between them. "Has he done this before?"

"No. Never."

He glanced at his watch. "It's only five o'clock, so we've got a good three hours or so of sunlight left. I'll take a walk around outside, make sure he's not just sulking behind the garage, while you make a few phone calls, all right?"

"Thank you."

Caleb gave her shoulder a squeeze, winked at Emma, and then disappeared out the back door. Lauren raced to the phone.

Caleb found him at the mini-mart playing an ancient pinball machine with a black-haired boy about the same age, maybe older. Hard to tell since Max was quite big for his age.

Neither boy saw Caleb approach. He walked up and laid an arm across the back of the machine.

"Bonanza pinball? Huh, who'da thunk it? I mean, this thing must be thirty years old, at least."

"It was made in 1964," the balding, middle-aged man behind the counter informed him. "Got it for a song down in Milwaukee." He grinned, revealing a broken front tooth, before returning his attention to the portable TV behind him.

"So, who's winning?"

Max and his friend exchanged looks. His friend shrugged.

"Who the heck are you, and why are you following me?" Max demanded.

"Why did you leave without telling your mother where you were going?" Caleb countered.

"None of your business, old man!"

Old man? Boy, this kid needed an old-fashioned, over-the-knee ass-whooping. "I'm a friend of your mother's."

Max rolled his eyes. "Yeah, a friend. Okay. Call it what you want, but stay out of my business."

Caleb dropped his arm from the top of the pinball machine and took a step forward. Uncertainty flashed in Max's eyes, but then the little punk found his smart mouth again. "I ain't afraid of you...my dad's bigger'n you."

"Yeah? Well, I don't see your dad around anywhere, do you?" Caleb knew it was a low blow, but this kid needed a reality check. Caleb knew better than anyone what Max was going through, what he was feeling.

"He'll be back," Max said, although his tone lacked conviction.

"He'd be a fool if he didn't come back. Listen, your mom's worried sick, so why don't we put her out of her misery and get you home?"

Max crossed his arms in defiance. "I ain't going nowhere with you." A smug grin curved his lips. "You're a stranger, and my mom told me never to get in the car with strangers."

Caleb couldn't help but respect the little stinker's brass. But enough was enough. "If you don't come with me right now, I'll throw you over my knee in front of God and anyone else who cares to watch and give you the spanking of your life," Caleb promised in a low voice.

Max's eyes grew round with fear. His friend swallowed hard and backed up a step. "Dude, I'm outta here," he said before taking off like a shot, the bell over the door tinkling in his wake.

Caleb clapped Max on the back. "Let's go. Now."

Max's face screwed up in a scowl, but he wisely followed Caleb from the store.

They rode in silence for a few minutes, Max staring out the passenger side window of Caleb's black Chevy Silverado, no doubt thinking up ways to get even with him.

"Believe it or not, I know how you're feeling."

Max remained stubbornly silent.

"I was only a few years older than you when my old man took off. Left in the middle of the night like a coward. Never said goodbye, love you, I'll be back. And I blamed my mom, just like you blame yours."

Max fidgeted in his seat, but still, not a word. Caleb made a right onto Willow Drive and pulled into Lauren's driveway. He parked the car, but instead of getting out, he turned to face Max. "It's not your mom's fault your dad left, and I think deep down you know that. Maybe you could cut her a break on the attitude."

Max lifted angry eyes to Caleb, but kept his mouth shut.

Lauren stepped out onto the porch and shielded her eyes from the glare of the evening sun. She dropped her hand as Max got out of the truck, and Caleb found breathing impossible as the most beautiful smile he'd ever seen lit up her face.

Caleb got out, too, but hung back as Max approached his mother.

Lauren tried to hug him, but the kid stormed past her into the house. Caleb strode up to the porch and took her into his arms. She hung onto him as if for dear life. It struck him that they'd only met that morning, yet he'd never felt more comfortable with anyone before, male or female. The thought startled him and he pulled back slightly. "You okay?"

She blew out a shaky breath and nodded. "You'd think I'd be used to it by now, you know? It's been almost a year since I"—she made the quote signs—"ruined his life. I keep telling myself he'll get over it, but what if he doesn't? What if my little boy who hates me turns into a grown man who hates me?"

Caleb smiled reassuringly. "I promise he'll get over it. Trust me."

Loud music suddenly blared through the front door, and Lauren rolled her eyes.

"You want me to take care of this for you?" Caleb asked. He let go of her hands and stepped back.

"I appreciate the offer, but no. I need to take care of this myself."

He nodded his understanding. "Thanks again for supper. Call you tomorrow?"

"I'd like that."

Caleb was trying to decide whether or not to kiss her when the front door flew open and Emma waddled out. "Momma, Max a bad boy! He call me soopid baby!"

She swung Emma up into her arms, and Caleb's heart melted like butter on a biscuit as the two most beautiful girls in Redemption smiled up at him. He gave one of Emma's honey curls a gentle tug, winked at Lauren, and got the hell out of there while he still could.

Lauren watched Caleb drive away with a sense of regret. She was almost sure he'd been about to kiss her when Emma barreled through the door. She kissed her daughter's cheek. "Lucky I adore you, Little Miss Rotten Timing."

"'Dore you, too, Momma." Emma wrapped her arms around Lauren's neck.

Lauren carried her inside, settled her in front of the TV, and headed up the stairs to confront her son. He was lying on his bed, hands clasped behind his head and eyes closed. Lauren strode across the room and turned off his stereo. Max opened his eyes and glared at her. "Hey, I was listening to that!"

Lauren walked over and sat on the edge of his bed.

"Max, we have to talk about this."

"What's to talk about? My dad's gone and you..."

His words trailed off, and Lauren waited for him to continue, surprised the insults weren't being hurled quite as fast as usual. She had to constantly remind herself how hard it must have been for him to lose his father like that. And without so much as a letter or a phone call in all these months. Of course, John Frazier had never been much of a father, but she never could've imagined he'd abandon his own children like this. "And I...?"

"Forget it." Max closed his eyes, tuning her out.

"I can't forget it, and you know it." Lauren blew out a hard breath and eased up off the bed. "Look, I know it's easier to blame me since your father isn't here, but I'm really tired of you using your sister and me as your personal punching bags. Your father left us, Max. All three of us, not just you. And in case you're wondering, I'll never leave you. You're stuck with me, kiddo."

His eyes remained closed. "I know, all right? Just leave me alone. I wanna be alone."

Frustrated, Lauren backed out of his bedroom and closed the door. She rushed into the bathroom, locked herself inside, and let her emotions have the floor. She sobbed silently, a wad of toilet paper clutched in her fist.

God, how she hated her ex-husband. John Frazier deserved to be boiled in oil for what he'd done to them, especially his son. How could a man just up and leave his children without so much as a word? And then disappear from the face of the earth? Oh, Lauren knew she could find his sorry ass if she wanted to hire a PI. But since that plan would require taking a second mortgage out on her home, it was never going to happen. Somehow, she knew it would be worse for Max if his father were dragged back kicking and screaming. They were all better off without him, and that was a fact. Her kids deserved much better than the likes of John Frazier. They deserved someone steady and true.

Someone like…Caleb Hunter.

Chapter Three

"Are you sure it was Max?" Lauren clutched the phone to her ear and prayed for patience as Mr. Collier from down the road explained how he'd caught Max and two of his friends throwing eggs at his house. He'd given chase, but they'd gotten away.

"I'm sure. Listen, I don't plan to press charges, but if I catch him again, I'm calling the cops."

"As you should. I'm so sorry, Mr. Collier. And of course, I'll pay for any damage." Her stomach lurched at the thought of another debt.

"There's no damage, young lady. I just need to get the hose out and wash the brick."

"I'll send Max down to help as soon as I find him." If I find him, she thought, tempted to call the police herself.

Mr. Collier let out a snorting laugh. "Please don't. Just find him before he does some real damage." And he hung up.

Lauren packed Emma into the car, and then started combing the neighborhood for her wayward son. She felt so helpless, so frightened. Max's antics were getting worse by the day, and she had no idea what to do to help him. All she knew for certain was if she didn't nip this destructive crap in the bud soon, Max would find himself sitting in a jail cell with a one-way ticket to juvy hall.

By the time she found him—hanging out in front of the hardware store with his friend, Eddie, and two boys she'd never seen before—Lauren was ready to drag him home by his ear.

"Maxwell Frazier, you get in this car right now," she said through her teeth. Max swung around and, at first, seemed shocked to see her. But then his new friends razzed him a bit, and a scowl replaced his doe-eyed expression.

"I'll be home later," he snapped, while his friends snickered and offered comments she, thankfully, couldn't hear.

Lauren angrily blinked back tears. Without thinking, she swung the door open, but quickly realized she couldn't leave Emma alone. Max knew she wouldn't give chase with Emma in the car, so he turned his back on her, effectively dismissing her.

"Momma, Max bad boy," Emma informed her in all seriousness, which would've been funny under normal circumstances.

Lauren blew out a frustrated breath and put the car in gear. Before she could turn out onto Main Street, someone tapped on her window, scaring the bejesus out of her.

"I'm sorry, didn't mean to startle you." Caleb leaned down to wink at Emma. "Hey, punkin."

"Ca'yib! Max bad boy 'gin. He make Momma cry."

Lauren put the car back in park, then turned and shook her head at the little stinker. "Tattletale."

Caleb's expression hardened. He cast a look at Max and his friends, who were all openly staring at Caleb, and then reached in and cupped Lauren's cheek. "I'll handle this, if you like."

Lauren was somewhat surprised by the intimate touch. But in a good way. She'd love to close her eyes and snuggle into his warm palm. "I'd like very much. But if you help me drag him back home, he'll just run out again. He'll also resent you ten times more than he already does."

Caleb waved that off. "He'll get over it. I'm more worried about what he'll do in the meantime. I've been in Max's shoes. He's got a lot of anger brewing inside of him. Mixed with adolescent angst, that's a lethal combination."

"Okay, not helping," Lauren said, her fear escalating.

Before Caleb could respond, a rock whizzed past the windshield, followed by a second, which just missed his head. Caleb dropped to a crouch and let out a curse. "Stay in the car," he ordered.

Lauren watched in horror as Caleb gave chase. All four boys split up and ran in different directions, but Caleb raced after Max. And my God was he fast. Lauren watched with her mouth hanging open as Caleb caught Max by the collar before he'd even reached the edge of the hardware store's parking lot. She opened her door and got out of the car, tempted to run over and intervene, but the fact that Emma was in the car kept her rooted firmly in place.

"Let me go! You got no right touching me. I'm a minor! You stupid, son-of-a—"

Caleb clamped a hand over Max's mouth, and escorted him to Lauren's car. He yanked the back door open, but before he took his hand from Max's mouth, he warned, "One cuss word, and you'll regret it."

Max met Lauren's gaze, his eyes red-rimmed and filled with disgust. "I hate you," he seethed.

Caleb stuffed him in the backseat and ordered, "Put your seatbelt on." Caleb shut the door and caught Lauren's eye. He hooked a thumb toward the hardware store. "I have to go pick up a few things for a job tomorrow. I'll be by as soon as I'm done. Think you'll be all right?"

Lauren had no idea what to say. Or what to think. Could it really have been just yesterday Caleb Hunter walked through her front door and into her life? In some ways, it felt as if she'd known him forever. It was such a relief to have help with Max. Her mother lived halfway across the country in sunny California, and her father had cut ties with her when his new wife gave him an ultimatum: her or Lauren. Frankly, Lauren had been less than surprised by his choice.

"I'll be fine, thanks." She lowered her voice. "Listen, you don't have to come by. I feel like I've taken up so much of your time already. This is my problem, I'll deal with it."

"You shouldn't have to deal with it alone," he replied in a low tone. "He's a big boy, Lauren. If he got physical with you, think you'd be able to handle him?"

Lauren bit down on her bottom lip. Max was her son, her little boy. He'd never hurt her, of that she was certain. He did need some male guidance, however, and Caleb was the only man who'd ever shown any interest in her kids.

"Can we just go?" Max whined from the backseat.

Lauren made a quick decision. If Caleb was willing to help her rein Max in, get his anger under control, she'd be foolish to turn down his generosity. And of course it had nothing to do with the fact that the man was gorgeous, or that she craved his company like most women craved chocolate.

Steely determination stiffened her spine. "I'll be fine, don't worry."

"So, spill. Who's the handsome stranger I saw fixing your front door yesterday?"

Lauren's next-door neighbor, Carrie Lowell, handed Lauren a loaf of still warm zucchini bread and strode past her into the house. Once they were seated at the kitchen table, Lauren poured them each a cup of coffee and cut them each a slice of the bread. Carrie had been Lauren's rock those first few weeks after John had left. Having gone through a divorce herself, she'd known exactly what to say and what not to say, simply listening when Lauren needed to vent, and holding her when she'd needed to cry.

"His name's Caleb Hunter. Matt sent him over for a haircut, and the house decided to start dropping parts while he was here."

Carrie chuckled. "It's just its way of saying hello."

Lauren grinned. "Well, yesterday, it was in an especially friendly mood. And Caleb, out of pity, offered to do a few repairs in exchange for a home-cooked meal."

"Uh-huh. For a home-cooked meal. I'm sure it had nothing to do with the fact you're supermodel gorgeous."

Lauren rolled her eyes. "Yeah, that's me, Heidi Klum's twin. Anyway, he fixed the front and back doors, then Max's bottom drawer that's been stuck shut. Only Max wasn't too happy to find a stranger in his room when he got home."

"I'll bet." Carrie took a sip of her coffee. "So did this Caleb go running for the hills after he met Max?"

Lauren broke off a small piece of the moist bread and popped it in her mouth. "That's the surprising part—no. When Max didn't come down for supper, I went up to get him and discovered he'd snuck out of the house. Caleb went out, found him, and dragged him home."

Carrie's brow shot up. "Wow, a real man. Didn't think there were any of those left in the world."

Lauren gave an absent nod. She didn't quite share her friend's cynical views on the male population, but understood where she was coming from. "When he said he'd call, believe me, I had doubts. Then yesterday, Max took off again. I found him hanging out in front of the hardware store with some punks I'd never seen before, and Caleb showed up." Lauren shared the entire story with her.

Carrie made a face. "Sounds a little too good to be true, if you ask me."

"I know, right? My thoughts exactly. But Max is exhausting, and I'm scared to death of what he'll do next. Yesterday I got a call from Mr. Collier. He caught Max and those punks throwing eggs at his house. That's why I went looking for him." Lauren blew out a shaky breath, took a sip of her coffee. "Caleb made a comment about having been in Max's shoes. He didn't elaborate, but I got the impression his own father pulled a disappearing act, too. Maybe he's exactly what Max needs, someone who understands how he—" Lauren stopped and gave her head a rueful shake. "Is it terrible of me to let this man, this...virtual stranger, take on my burdens?"

Carrie's eyes softened. "Of course not. You're human, and you have a lot on your plate right now."

Lauren absently picked at her zucchini-raisin bread. "Yeah, but who doesn't. I'm just desperate for help with Max. He's drowning in his misery, and I have no idea how to help him. But maybe Caleb does, you know? Or maybe I'm just a terrible mother."

"Do I need to slap some sense into you? Come on, Laur, you're a wonderful mother. And there's nothing shameful about admitting you need help, or accepting help when it's offered."

Lauren had to blink back tears. Normally, she wasn't this weepy and emotional. Her period must be due, she thought with a rueful eye roll. "Thanks, I can always count on you to put things into perspective. And since I invited Caleb to supper again tonight," she continued with a grin, "your speech came at just the right moment."

Carrie laughed. "Glad I could help." Suddenly, her expression sobered. "Hey, did you hear about Rosalee?"

"No, what about her?"

"She passed away a few weeks back. Heard it was a heart attack."

Fresh tears stung Lauren's eyes. "My God, poor Hutch." Lauren and the kids adored Rosalee, who'd been a waitress at Hutch's Diner for years; long before Lauren and her ex had moved to Redemption. Rosalee and Hutch had been planning to get married this summer…Max and Emma were going to be heartbroken when she told them. "Life really is short, isn't it?" she murmured.

"It sure is. So quit doubting yourself and start putting your own needs out there, too. Caleb may or may not be what Max needs, but he sure as hell seems to be exactly what you need."

"Wow, is this déjà vu or what?" Lauren teased as Caleb walked in the front door. He had his tool belt strapped on his hips, and a sexy grin on his lips.

"Cute."

She laughed. "Perfect timing. Supper's ready."

Caleb unhooked his tool belt and hung it on the coat tree. "Smells delicious." He followed her into the kitchen. "Keep feeding me like this and you'll never get rid of me."

That's the plan, Stan. "Don't worry, this house needs so much work, you won't eat a frozen pizza for months."

Caleb met her gaze, a slow smile lifting the corners of his lips. "Can I get that in writing?"

"Ca'yib!"

Lauren's heart swelled when Emma hobbled into the kitchen, straight into Caleb's arms. For a split second, she wondered if it was wise allowing her daughter to become so attached to a man they'd only just met. For all Lauren knew, she and Caleb might prove to be completely incompatible.

Caleb swung Emma up and propped her on his hip, like an old pro. "And how's the prettiest little girl in Redemption doing?"

"I helped Momma cook. We make pork chops and corn."

"Wow, beautiful and a good cook, just like your mommy. You're going to make some lucky guy very happy one day."

Lauren playfully rolled her eyes as she took Emma from him. "One day way, way in the future," she teased as she settled her in her high chair.

"Max!" Emma squealed.

Lauren swung her head around, and sure enough, Max stood at the bottom of the stairs, gaze wary, arms crossed and shoulders hunched. He cast Caleb a dismissive glance before walking around to take his usual seat at the table, directly across from where Caleb sat.

"I'm glad you decided to join us," she said. "I made those brown and serve rolls you like so much."

Max gave a curt nod to indicate he'd heard her, but that was it.

Caleb met her gaze and quirked a brow, but Lauren shook her head, so he remained silent. Max was sitting at the dinner table with them, and for now, that was enough.

Lauren would take any little bit of forward progress she could and be grateful for it.

If not for Emma, they would have eaten in virtual silence. Besides her happy chattering, the only sounds to be heard were the scraping of silverware on plates and ice clinking in glasses. Lauren's hope grew when Max stayed and ate chocolate cake with them. And the whole meal was eaten without one single insult leaving his lips. For the first time in months, Lauren felt a glimmer of optimism.

"Well…" Caleb pushed his chair back. "Guess I'd better go earn my supper. What do you have next on the agenda?"

Caleb spent the next two hours shaving a good chunk off her 'to fix' list. And Lauren started to feel like a couple of dinners just weren't payment enough for all the work he'd done. Not to mention his help with Max. That alone was worth a whole lifetime of home-cooked goodness as far as she was concerned.

Whoa…a whole lifetime? Hell, you don't even know if the man's a good kisser yet.

He came up behind her and rested his hands on her shoulders. Lauren flinched; he dropped his hands. "Sorry. Didn't mean to scare you."

She turned to face him and gave her head a self-conscious shake. "No, it's all me. I was lost in thought."

"Turn around."

"Huh?"

Caleb chuckled. He gently turned her so she was facing away from him again, then grasped her shoulders and started kneading.

Lauren closed her eyes as a low groan of contentment reverberated in her throat. She couldn't remember the last time she'd gotten a massage, and Lord did it feel heavenly. After about thirty seconds, she knew she had to stop him before she melted into a puddle on the floor. She opened her eyes—and met her son's harsh gaze. He spun around and raced up the stairs.

"Max!" Lauren tore free of Caleb's magic fingers. She heard a door slam and stood helpless, unsure whether she should race up after him, or leave well enough alone and let him sulk in peace.

"He's going through a difficult time. It's hard for a young boy to understand why his father would up and leave him. And even worse when they don't call or write."

Lauren turned to glare up at him. "You think I don't know that? That I'm clueless when it comes to my own son and need you to explain him to me?"

"I didn't mean—"

Lauren took a deep, shuddering breath. "It's been a year since John left. He could be dead for all I know, and frankly, for all I care. But my son cares. I live every day in fear that if John doesn't contact us soon, Max will blame me forever...hate me forever. Do you have any idea what that feels like?"

Caleb propped his hands on his hips and dropped his gaze to the floor. "Look, I didn't mean to upset you, only to help. I'd best get going."

When he turned to leave, Lauren's anger expelled in a big whoosh as she realized she was about to chase away the only person, besides Carrie, who'd ever shown an interest in her kids. "Please don't. I'm so sorry. I-I just need a day at the spa or something." She tried to laugh, but it came out more of a croaky sob.

Caleb turned back around and pulled her into his arms. "Lady, what is it about you?" he whispered against her cheek.

Lauren snuggled into his embrace, soaking him in like a dry sponge, wanting nothing more than to stay in his arms forever. But reality reared its ugly head, and she knew she couldn't indulge herself for long. Not with Max so upset upstairs. "Caleb, I need to go talk to him. I know he's a big boy, but he's still only ten years old and doesn't understand why I would let someone besides his father...touch me."

He pulled back and cleared his throat. "If you need anything..."

"I know. And thank you. For everything. I'll talk to you soon, I promise."

His gaze dropped to her lips, and for a moment Lauren thought he would kiss her. But they both knew the time wasn't right, so with obvious regret, he stepped back and said, "Call me if you need anything."

Chapter Four

Caleb stood staring down at his mother's grave, his heart heavy with guilt, his throat swollen with repressed grief. She'd been asking for him to visit more often the past couple of years, never pressing too hard, just casual comments like, "Sure wish your job allowed you to travel more." Or "So, you seeing anyone special? I'd love to meet her." How sadly ironic that when he finally finds a woman who intrigues him like no other, she lives only a few miles from his mother's home.

Crouching down, he blew out a shaky breath. Rosalee Hunter, Beloved Mother. Christ, what he wouldn't give to be able to turn back time and do it all again. Make better choices, be less judgmental, more forgiving. Be the kind of son she'd deserved.

If he'd visited more often, he'd have met Lauren sooner and his mother could've known her. A smile touched his lips. His mother would've loved Emma. And she would've turned herself inside out trying to help Max cope with the loss of his father.

Just as she'd done for Caleb.

He reached out and ran a reverent finger across the words etched in marble. If Caleb hadn't been busy holding grudges, he probably would've been there when she'd had her massive heart attack. Maybe he would've had a chance to say all the things he should've said years ago. Maybe he'd have gotten one last, long overdue "I love you" in there.

Caleb kissed his fingers and pressed them to his mother's name. He stood and flexed his hands, feeling incredibly uncomfortable in his own skin. *A day late and a dollar short. Just like you always said, Mom.*

The last few rays of sunlight faded into the western horizon as Caleb walked back to his truck. He needed a drink. Maybe two. Just to take the edge off. And he hadn't been inside Rowdy's in years. Besides, if he went back to the house in this frame of mind, he'd probably lapse into a state of depression—like he had when he'd returned home from active duty.

He passed Hutch's Diner and couldn't help taking a quick glance inside before pulling into Rowdy's parking lot across the street. Caleb sat for a moment, fingers laced on the steering wheel, watching as Hutch Hutchinson poured a cup of coffee for a customer. *Maybe the time's come to forgive.* With a silent sigh, Caleb grabbed his keys and climbed out of the truck, ignoring the urge to spin around and head to Hutch's place instead.

As soon as he yanked open the door, a feeling of familiarity overcame him. A welcome feeling, much to his surprise. The place looked the same, as far as he could remember: plenty of beer paraphernalia covering the walls; signs, mirrors, a clock with a moving waterfall. A country love song played on the jukebox, and Caleb's gaze was drawn to the young couple dancing in the corner, held tight in each other's arms while they swayed to the music. A wistful feeling tightened his chest, and he imagined slow-dancing with Lauren, her beautiful blue eyes gazing up at him, full of love and ablaze with promise.

Jesus, Hunter, get a grip. You've only known the lady three days. He blinked the image away, gave himself a mental shake, and proceeded toward the bar. Caleb slid onto a stool and folded his arms on the counter. The tallest woman he'd ever seen strolled toward him, and he found himself sitting up a little straighter. As she drew near, he realized she had piercings in her face. Now there was one thing Caleb would never understand, someone wanting to punch a hole through their nose.

"Evening." She set a bowl of pretzels in front of him. "What can I get you?"

"Give me a shot of Christian Brothers, if you have it, and a bottle of Bud."

She retrieved a familiar bottle from the top shelf behind her, a shot glass from beneath the bar, and poured him a healthy splash. Caleb tossed the shot back just as she set his beer down in front of him.

"Thanks." He dug a twenty out of his wallet and tossed it on the bar.

After making his change, she tilted her head to the side. "I don't think I've seen you in here before. You new in town?"

Caleb took a pull on his beer, resisting the urge to glance back at the dancing couple. "No, I grew up here. Joined the Army after high school and haven't been back much since."

"Well, let's hope you're here to stay this time." She gave him a wink before strolling off to take care of some other customers.

Caleb nursed his beer, his head a jumble of thoughts. He planned to take the electrician's exam on Monday, and knew he was as prepared as he'd ever be. He'd been taking odd jobs around town since after his mother's funeral, and thanks to word-of-mouth, his phone had been ringing off the hook with people in need of his services. The time had come to make a decision about his future—stay in Redemption or head back to Chicago.

Until a few days ago, he'd been leaning toward Chicago, even if he'd never been especially happy there. But it had been home for so long, and he'd made a few friends over the years. Then he'd met Lauren and his whole perspective changed—which scared the living shit out of him. The possibility of a happily-ever-after suddenly seemed real and within reach. He'd never been one to believe in love at first sight, but what else could explain the soul-deep awareness that had cold-cocked him the first time he'd laid eyes on her?

Or maybe it was something more basic, the rational part of his brain reasoned. He was thirty-four years old. Never married, no children. Maybe men had internal clocks, too, and his days of hitting the snooze button were coming to an end. Time to settle down and start a family before he was too old to enjoy them.

But a ready-made family? Not too long ago the thought would've terrified him. Now, much to his amazement, not so much. He could easily imagine waking up next to Lauren every day for the next fifty years. And Max and Emma deserved better than a father who'd slunk off in the middle of the night like a coward. A father who couldn't be bothered to call his own children, let them know where he was, why he left, and when—or if—he'd be back.

Max needed a father who would love and guide him, teach him what it means to be a man, not a coward who runs out on the people who need him most. Teach him that a real man respects women; he doesn't take advantage of them physically or emotionally.

Emma, on the other hand, needed unconditional love and support. Too young to have any lasting memories of her father, she was a clean slate, and whoever she ended up calling daddy would be a lucky man indeed. Those children deserved the best, and so did Lauren. But was Caleb that man? Was he ready to become a father to those children?

Jesus, Hunter, jumping the gun a little here, or what?

"Hey, Marv, isn't that the same kid from last week?"

Caleb turned to see who the bartender referred to, and there stood Max, feeding money into the cigarette machine. Caleb should've been surprised to see him, but wasn't. Good God, couldn't the kid give his mother one friggin' night's peace?

"Yup, that's the one," Caleb heard from behind him.

"Thought so. I'll go grab the little punk, you call the cops."

Caleb rose up and turned to face them. "Listen, I know the kid's mother, and she's had a pretty bad time of it lately. Let me take him home, and I promise you won't see him in here again."

Marv and the Amazon woman exchanged looks. Marv shrugged. "Fine. But if I see him in here again, I'm calling the cops."

Caleb nodded. "Appreciate it." He left his change on the bar and strode across the room until he was standing right behind the little shit. "I thought I told you these things are bad for you."

Max jumped almost a foot in the air. When he recognized Caleb, he let out a curse and stuffed his money back in his pocket. "Why won't you leave me alone? I'm tired of you following me around town, like a stalker or something."

"Hate to burst your bubble, kid, but I was in here first. And I'd be a little nicer to me if I were you. I just saved you from getting hauled off to jail."

Max rolled his eyes and started toward the door. "Whatever."

Caleb grabbed his arm. "No, not whatever. I'm taking you home, let's go." Once they were outside, Caleb said, "Christ, don't you care about your mother at all?"

"It's none of your business how I feel," Max muttered, trying to wrench his arm free.

Caleb opened the passenger-side door and shoved Max in the truck. "Don't forget your seat belt."

"Why?" Max shot back. "If I die, you won't have to worry about me getting in your way with my mom."

Caleb walked around to the driver's side and climbed in behind the wheel. Max's statement reminded him of just how young the boy was, despite appearances. He took a deep breath and started up the truck. "Son, I don't want anything to happen to you. I'd like to help, if you'll let me."

Max stared straight ahead, but Caleb recognized a trace of vulnerability shadowed in the kid's expression. Caleb's throat swelled with unfamiliar emotion. Somehow, the kid had burrowed under his skin, making Caleb feel things he was completely unprepared to deal with. Hell, so had his mother and sister. Christ, he was a goner on so many levels it wasn't funny. But he could sort all that shit out later. Right now, the only thing he cared about was breaking through the wall of rage Max had built up around himself over the past year.

Caleb pulled out his cell phone and called Lauren. Turned out Max had snuck out of the house again, and Lauren had been on the verge of panic.

"I'm just so glad you were there. I'm starting to think kismet isn't just a pretty word."

Despite her attempt to sound composed, Caleb knew this was killing her. He also knew he didn't have the right to butt into their lives, but Max needed guidance and Lauren needed help—even if she was too stubborn to admit it. An idea occurred to him. "Listen, would it be all right if I took Max to my place for a little while? I could use some help with a project I've been working on, and I think he'd be perfect for the job."

A slight pause. "I don't know. It's pretty late, and I'm already so far in debt to you. I'll be feeding you supper 'til Emma's in high school."

"Just an hour. I'll have him home by nine thirty."

Max shot Caleb a quick look, but remained silent.

"Can you put him on the phone, please?"

Caleb held out the phone. "Say hello to your mother."

Max ignored Caleb's outstretched hand. "Hello to your mother."

Smart-mouthed little crapper. Caleb put the phone back to his ear. "Sorry about that. You deserve better."

"I'm getting used to his disrespect," she replied, a shrug in her voice. "Fine, one hour. And Caleb, I don't know what else to say but thanks…again."

Caleb ended the call, cast his sullen passenger a quick look, then put the truck in gear and headed home.

"You really made this?"

Caleb ran his hand over the wooden sign that read Lauren's Hair Salon. "Yep. Think she'll like it?"

Max stared at the sign, his expression guarded. Finally, he gave a reluctant nod.

"Good, I wasn't sure. I still need to stain and weatherproof it. Thought maybe you could give me a hand."

Max looked up at him. "I don't know how to do that kind of stuff."

"I'll teach you. It's easy." Caleb set the wooden sign down on his workbench and opened the can of stain. After a good stir, he selected a brush, dipped it in the can, and scraped the excess off on the inside of the rim. "Now, you just brush it on, making sure to cover every square inch. Think you can handle it?"

Max gave him a "duh" look and held his hand out for the brush. Caleb could barely contain his smile as Max took the brush and went to work.

"The sign is carved on both sides," Caleb explained, pleased by Max's eye for detail as he worked the brush into the grooves. "So both sides will have to be stained. And instead of hanging it back on the house, I thought it would look sharp hanging from a post in the front yard." A grin tugged at Caleb's mouth. "Maybe I should've made sure your mom's okay with me digging in the yard, first."

Max eyed him as he reapplied stain to the brush. "She won't care, trust me. She'll probably start crying when she sees it. Just warning ya."

Caleb lost the battle with the grin. "Thanks for the heads up."

Once Max had the first side finished, Caleb said, "We'll give this a few minutes to dry before flipping it over. Come on." He opened the door that led into the house.

"What?"

"I picked up some double-chocolate caramel brownies from the grocery store today. Thought you might want to try 'em out with me."

Max shrugged and started forward, his steps hesitant.

"Might wanna move faster than that," Caleb warned as he stepped inside. "I can eat a dozen brownies in about thirty seconds flat." The quick staccato of footsteps brought an odd ache to his chest as Max hurried in behind him and took a seat at the butcher block and white finish wood kitchen table.

Max looked around with open-mouthed curiosity, and Caleb found himself strangely eager for the kid's approval. The kitchen was done in shades of yellow, white, red and blue, in what his mother had called "country charm."

Lots of stars and hearts, crafts made of wood, buttons, and colored twine. As a kid, Caleb hadn't much appreciated the homey look. As an adult, he found it as comforting as...chicken bake. He smiled and hoped it wasn't goofy.

Caleb set the brownies in the middle of the table and poured them each a glass of milk. Guys didn't need plates and napkins and forks. Just more stuff that needed washing. They both dug in and grabbed one of the gooey, crumbling brownies.

They ate in silence for several minutes before Max got up and went to look at something on the refrigerator. A photo of Caleb and his mother taken shortly before he'd enlisted in the army.

He turned to study Caleb, then back to the photo.

"Hey, is Rosalee your mom?"

Caleb nodded, surprised by the question. "Did you...how did you know my mother?"

"We used to go to the diner after my guitar lessons." Max walked back to the table and grabbed another brownie.

"I had no idea you played guitar."

Max nodded as he chewed. He took a gulp of his milk. "I quit taking lessons, so we don't go to the diner anymore. Your mom's cool. She always lets me keep the can of whipped cream on the table when I order hot chocolate."

"Sounds like her." His mother had known Lauren and the kids. The thought pleased him, somewhat easing the guilt he'd been carrying around like a backpack. Then Max's words registered. "Max, you do know my mother passed away a short time ago, don't you?"

Max looked up, his shock evident.

"What? No, I...God, I'm really sorry."

"Yeah, me too. But I'm glad you knew her."

"Rosalee's…was the best." Max settled his gaze back on the picture. "I don't think my mom knows. She's gonna be super bummed."

Caleb nodded, wondering suddenly if his mother had ever spoken about him to Lauren.

He and Max sat in silence for a moment. One last brownie sat in the tray. Caleb pushed it toward Max's side of the table. "Go on, take it."

"Cool, thanks." Max scooped it up without a moment's hesitation.

Caleb grinned. "You earned it. When you're done, we'll finish up that sign. I'd like to put it up for your mother tomorrow."

"Why're you being so nice to me?" Max asked once he'd polished off the last brownie. "I know you don't like me, and it's not like my mom cares what I think, anyway."

Caleb gulped down the rest of his milk, then got up to put the glass in the sink. He turned and leaned back against the sink, arms crossed, making sure to choose his words carefully. "Your mother cares very much what you think, Max. Maybe if you took the time to actually talk to her instead of snapping at her, you'd have figured that out by now."

"She chased my dad away." Max's soft-spoken announcement surprised Caleb.

The kid sounded so dejected, so young, Caleb's heart went out to him. "Look, son, I know it's easier to blame your mom for what happened than—"

"But I heard her! I heard her tell him to pack his stuff and get out." Max's eyes grew red and angry. "You think I'm lying?"

"No, I don't doubt that's what you heard. But you have to understand, Max, she had reason. And just because she wanted him out of the house, didn't mean she wanted him out of your lives. Your father chose to leave, and your mother chose to stay. Maybe you should consider that next time you're trying to make her feel like crap."

Max's chin started to quiver. "I wanna go home."

Caleb took a deep breath. Good going, moron. Next, why don't you tell the kid his daddy hates him? "Look, I'm sorry. I had no right talking about your dad. I just want you to consider how hard this has been on your mother. Maybe give her a break now and then."

"You don't understand." Max got up and headed back into the garage. Caleb followed him. "We were supposed to go hunting this year. He said when I turned eleven, he'd take me hunting." Max uncapped the stain and started on the other side.

Caleb watched the kid move the brush across the wood, taking care to get in every nook and cranny. Maybe it would be best if they got off the subject of his parents. "You know, you're pretty darn good at that. Any chance you'd want to earn some extra money? I have several jobs coming up that involve staining."

The brush stopped. Caleb could see the wheels turning in Max's head. Caleb knew times were tight in the Frazier household, so it was a sure bet the kid could use the cash.

"How much would you pay me?"

"If your mom says it's all right, I'll give you eight bucks an hour."

"Cool."

Chapter Five

"*Y*ou what?"

Caleb smiled. "We made you a new sign. For your business."

"I stained the whole thing, both sides," Max proudly informed her. "'Cept the post. Caleb already had that done."

Lauren's chest filled with joy as she gazed at her seemingly happy son. Not only was Max speaking to her, but he was smiling as well. And all thanks to Caleb. "I don't know what to say. You guys are the best."

"So, it's all right if I dig up a hole for the post? I can hang the sign on the side of the house, if you prefer."

"No, I'd love to have it hanging in the yard. Wow, I think this has earned you guys a lasagna dinner."

Caleb grinned. "Garlic bread?"

"Apple pie, too. But not homemade," she admitted with a little shrug. "I have a Mrs. Smith's in the freezer."

Caleb elbowed Max. "Better let her out before she freezes to death, huh?"

Max chuckled, and the sound was music to Lauren's ears. She hadn't a clue what Caleb had said to her son, but she loved him for it.

Loved? Whoa.

Lauren cleared her throat. "Well, since I don't have any appointments this morning, I think I'll take Emma grocery shopping. I need a few things for supper."

"Take your time. I only had one job this morning, so maybe Max and I can try to scratch a few more things off your 'to fix' list."

"No complaints here."

By the time Lauren and Emma returned home, a gorgeous wooden sign, much fancier than she'd imagined, hung from an expertly carved L-shaped post in front of her house. Caleb came out and grabbed the bags, while Lauren unbuckled Emma from her car seat.

"It's absolutely beautiful. I don't even know what to say. It's worth so much more than a lasagna dinner."

Caleb came up behind her and whispered against her ear, "Maybe worth a kiss?"

Lauren's heart missed a beat. Luckily, she had a good grip on Emma. She met his gaze for a brief moment before walking past him into the house. Definitely worth a kiss.

And then some.

Caleb followed her into the kitchen and set the bags on the table. "I love lasagna. Trust me—I'm getting the better end of the deal here."

Lauren set Emma down and started putting away the groceries. "Then I'll graciously concede and get supper started. It'll be a couple of hours, at least. Is there anything you need to take care of before it's ready?"

Caleb flipped one of her kitchen chairs around and straddled it. He gazed up at her. "The only thing I'd like to do is get to know you better."

Hmmm, someone's grown a little bolder today. Lauren likes. "Sounds like a plan. You can keep me company while I get my sauce going."

"Homemade sauce?"

Lauren laughed softly. His voice had raised a whole octave. "Of course. It's not that hard to make. Your mom probably made her own sauce." Too late she realized her blunder. She set the fresh mushrooms on the counter and turned to face him. "I'm so sorry. I didn't mean to—"

"Hey, it's fine. And, yes, she made her own sauce. In fact, I've never tasted any to compare."

Lauren pulled out her cutting board and sliced into an onion. "Well, prepare to be blown away, Mr. Hunter. I think my sauce would make your mother proud."

"Oh, Caleb told you about Rosalee?" Max said as he wandered into the kitchen. He went straight for the fridge and pulled out the milk gallon jug filled with Kool-Aid. "Pretty sad she died. Rosalee was awesome."

Stunned, Lauren locked eyes on Caleb. "Rosalee was your mother?" When he nodded, she clapped a hand to her chest. "I can't believe I didn't make the connection, I'm so sorry. I just found out yesterday that she passed. The kids and I loved her. What an incredible lady."

Caleb's smile was bittersweet. "I'm so glad you and the kids got a chance to know her."

"She was awesome. Made the best strawberry pie in the world and always saved me a piece." Max poured himself a big glass of Kool-Aid, then shook the jug in Caleb's direction. "Want some?"

Lauren's head popped up in astonishment. Cripes, it was as if the kid had received a complete personality transplant overnight. The phrase "too good to be true" flashed in her mind, but she told it to take a hike.

"I'd love a glass, thanks."

Okay, if they started singing 'Kumbaya' she'd know for sure it was time to start looking for the hidden cameras.

Lauren pulled out her cast-iron skillet and gave it a generous coating of olive oil before tossing in the diced onion and Italian sausage. She listened as Caleb described the jobs he'd booked for the next couple of weeks or so. Cabinets to reface, shelves to build, a brand new kitchen counter and dishwasher for a lady just down the road. Lauren was a little envious over that one. She'd love to have a dishwasher, but would be too old to enjoy it by the time she could afford one. Caleb had also been contracted to replace the wooden fence around the daycare center, and to patch the roof of the VFW.

"Mom, is it okay if I work with Caleb until school starts? He's gonna pay me eight bucks an hour!"

Lauren cast Caleb a quick glance. "Well, I'm not sure. I don't want him doing anything dangerous." Sure would be nice for Max to earn some money, though. It broke her heart that she couldn't afford to spoil her children every now and again. And Max's attitude had undergone an astounding transformation in such a short time. Lauren couldn't deny that spending time with Caleb had been good for her son.

"Course not. I have a lot of jobs that require staining and varnishing, even some light painting. And the kid's a natural. Has a real talent for it."

Max preened in his chair, and Lauren couldn't hold back a smile. Her respect for the incredible man sitting in her kitchen grew even more. Her ex had never taken the time to teach his son a blessed thing. Hell, he'd never even so much as tossed a ball around with Max. Probably because the only thing the man excelled at was something a ten-year-old boy had no business knowing. "In that case, I think it's a great idea. Thank you."

Caleb shrugged. "Shame for talent like that to go to waste. In fact, I'd like to get him started tomorrow staining the boards for that fence. Maybe between the two of us, we can finish them in a day."

Emma waddled into the kitchen and headed for the back door. "Sandbox, Momma."

"Max, would you please take your sister outside to play for a little while?"

He let out an exaggerated sigh and whined, "Can't we just watch her from the window? It's not like she can get out of the yard."

Lauren propped a hand on her hip and gave him her fiercest don't-argue-with-me look. Max's shoulders slumped in resignation.

"Fine. But just for a little while." Max got up and herded Emma out the back door. "And if you throw any sand at me, playtime's over."

Lauren pulled a metal spatula out of the drawer and broke up the clumps of browning meat and onions. "So, just how long of a day were you planning to work?"

"Don't worry, honey, I won't overwork him. Besides, Max is a strong kid. A little physical labor will be good for him. Wear him out so he has less time for troublemaking."

A slow smile spread across her face as understanding dawned. She pointed at him with the spatula. "You're a genius. I should've had him pushing the vacuum all this time."

"I'm not sure vacuuming would've gone over well. Max is a growing boy. He needs male interests, not women's work." Caleb grinned.

Lauren regarded him through playfully narrowed eyes. "Watch it."

"Sorry." His tone suggested he wasn't the least bit repentant.

Lauren added crushed tomatoes, tomato paste, a little sugar, and plenty of spices to her pan, and then turned the flame down to simmer. Caleb watched in silence while she mixed two beaten eggs with some parmesan and ricotta cheese.

"So," he said, "tell me about your family. Got any brothers or sisters? Does your family live here in Redemption?"

"No brothers or sisters, my mother lives in California, and I rarely hear from her. My father is remarried, but he hasn't spoken to me since I disobeyed his direct order not to marry John. And the fact I don't get along with his wife doesn't help."

Caleb got up and strode across the kitchen, settling against the counter beside her with his arms and his work-booted feet crossed. Lauren couldn't help but admire the tight fit of his gray T-shirt as it stretched over lean abs and perfectly sculpted arms. She got the impression he wanted to say something, but he remained quiet, shifting a bit as he focused his gaze out the window into the backyard. He smiled, probably over something her silly little peanut did. Lauren's heart flipped at the thought, and she worried over how hard and fast she was falling for this man.

"I'm sorry about your dad, and for even bringing the subject up." He turned back to face her, his smile rueful. "Seems like I apologize to you a lot."

"You have nothing to apologize for. I didn't have to share that with you, if I didn't want to."

He reached up and gently fingered a stray curl out of her eyes. "So why did you?"

"I don't know." She gave a one-shoulder shrug. "I just feel like...you're easy to talk to." She smiled, thinking of his earlier revelation. "You remind me of your mother. Easygoing, friendly. I'll miss her."

"Me, too. I'm just glad she got a chance to know you. And the kids. I bet she adored Emma. Max already told me about the whipped cream bit."

"He lit up around her. Hard to believe we'll never see her again." When he didn't respond, she met his gaze, her heart heavy with empathy. "I'm sorry, I...probably need to quit talking."

"You didn't say anything wrong. I'm just suffering from a guilty conscience."

"Why? I mean...do you want to talk about it?"

Caleb blew out a hard breath, and for a moment she didn't think he would comment. "Just the usual stuff, I guess. Wish I'd visited more, wish I'd called more often."

"I'm sure Rosalee knew how much you loved her." Lauren smiled in what she hoped was a reassuring way. She stirred her sauce, then dug her big aluminum pot out of the cabinet and began filling it with water.

Caleb nodded, though he seemed less than convinced. Lauren wondered if maybe it went deeper than he was letting on. "Thanks." He nodded toward the stove. "So, you need help with anything?"

A bloodcurdling scream rent the air. "Emma!" Lauren smacked the faucet down and raced out the back door, Caleb right on her heels.

Emma sat curled up in the grass, sobbing her heart out, while Max hovered over her frantically insisting, "Let me see 'em, Em! Come on, I have to see how bad it is!"

"How bad what is?" Lauren demanded as she dropped to her knees beside her baby and tried to figure out where she was hurt.

Caleb grabbed Max by the arm and helped him to his feet. "Come on, son, let your mother in there."

Lauren pulled Emma onto her lap. "Sweetheart, you have to calm down and tell me what happened," she crooned. "Show Momma, honey."

Emma lifted a shaky hand up for Lauren's inspection, her hysterical cries winding down to hiccupping sobs. Lauren had to hold back a sob of her own when she saw the condition of her daughter's fingers. The skin was cherry red with black bits stuck to her flesh that looked suspiciously like ashes.

Lauren shot Max a look as she scooped Emma into her arms. "What in the world happened? It looks like she burned her fingers." Without waiting for an answer, she ran back into the house and turned on the kitchen faucet. Emma screamed to the heavens when Lauren pressed her little fingers under the cool running water. Lauren had to bite her lip to keep her composure. Nothing in this world was worse than watching your child suffer. And Lord only knew how bad the damage was. But what could she have burned herself on? Had she found a pack of matches in the house somewhere?

"I'll drive you to the ER," Caleb said as he and Max entered behind her. "Wrap a clean dishtowel around her hand. Maybe apply some Vaseline or Neosporin first, if you have any."

He rushed over to the stove and turned off the burner, then asked Max to go grab Lauren's purse.

"How is she?" Caleb asked, peering over her shoulder.

Lauren cast him a quick glance. "Did you see anything lying in the grass? I'm afraid she may have found a pack of matches somewhere. I have a few in the drawer for when the stove pilot goes out."

Caleb rushed out the back door and returned a minute later, his expression grim. He held up a smoldering cigarette butt, which didn't make a lick of sense since Lauren didn't smoke. Neither did Carrie, or the Glockmans, who lived on the other side of her.

Caleb doused it in the sink and pitched it in the trash. "It'd be my guess she picked it up by the lit end, which would explain the charred bits stuck to her fingers."

Max finally showed up with his mother's purse and asked, "Is she all right?"

"Her fingers are burnt. Care to tell me how that happened?"

Max cast a quick, almost pleading glance at Caleb, who responded, "Come on, we'd better get Emma to the ER."

Chapter Six

———— ❧ ————

*O*nce Lauren and Emma were admitted into the
ER, Caleb clasped Max's shoulder. "Time to
tell me how Emma's fingers got burned."

He fed a dollar bill into the coffee machine
and pressed the button for hot chocolate. Christ,
if he'd told Lauren right away about the pack of
smokes he'd found in Max's "stuck" bottom
drawer, this never would've happened. And at
Rowdy's he'd been caught trying to buy a pack
of cigarettes, but again Caleb had given him the
benefit of the doubt. They'd made such progress
that night—Max had actually opened up to
him—Caleb had been sure the kid's self-
destructive phase was over, and there was no
reason to upset Lauren.

Guilt and frustration ate at him. That sweet little girl was in pain because of his poor choices. The urge to put his fist through the wall nearly overpowered him. He flexed his fingers and took a deep, calming breath before turning to face Max.

"It wasn't mine, I swear!"

"Sit down." Caleb held out the piping hot paper cup. "And be careful. Your mother couldn't handle another accident right now." Caleb sat down beside him. "Now tell me what happened, and don't even think about trying to con me."

"This dude named Bucky showed up and wanted me to go with him to the park to meet up with Eddie and Jimbo. When he lit up, I told him to put it out, but he wouldn't listen. Then he flicked it in the yard, and Emma ran over and picked it up before I could stop her." Max's face screwed up with anger. "Bucky's gonna be sorry when I catch up with him!"

Caleb sat down next to him. "Calm down. Let's just pray Emma's fingers aren't as bad as they looked."

"You believe me, don't you? I wasn't smoking." Looking into Max's eyes, Caleb had no doubt the boy was telling the truth. But it didn't lessen Caleb's own guilt. "I believe you.

But we have to tell your mother what happened."

"No way! She'll totally freak out, say I can't hang out with any of my friends anymore, give me some stupid curfew."

"You're ten, Max. You should have a curfew."

"Yeah, but she wants me in by eight o'clock. During the *summer*."

Caleb would've laughed if the situation hadn't been so dire.

Thirty minutes later, Lauren appeared through the double doors carrying a very sleepy Emma. Caleb watched with interest as one of the paramedics strode up to Lauren, his familiarity and concern unmistakable. After a short exchange, he gave Emma a kiss on the forehead, Lauren's shoulder a squeeze, and walked out of the hospital with his fellow EMTs.

Caught off guard by an overwhelming rush of jealousy, Caleb shot to his feet. His face grew hot and an unreasonable urge to race out after the guy and beat the hell out of him took hold. *So this is what the green-eyed monster feels like.* The unfamiliar emotion was not a welcome one.

Once they were in the car on the way home, Lauren touched his leg and said, "I want to thank you for jumping in and taking care of us. I don't know what I would've done if not for you."

"You would've handled the situation just fine. Luckily, Emma's burns weren't as bad as they looked."

"I know." She peeked over her shoulder at her sleeping daughter.

He was already attached to the lot of them, and it struck him with the force of a freight train that he had no idea how Lauren even felt about him. Jesus, he was half in love with her, and she may be feeling nothing more than gratitude. Caleb let his frustration out on a silent breath as he recalled the adoring way she'd gazed up at that paramedic.

"You okay?" Lauren asked him.

He shot her a quick glance, praying his expression didn't give away his inner turmoil. "Yeah. Just remembered I have a few phone calls to make when I get home."

"Oh. I'm sorry we kept you so long. I'd still plan to make the lasagna, but maybe we should save it for tomorrow?"

Caleb glanced back at Max who looked thoroughly miserable with his hangdog expression and slumped shoulders. While Caleb hated keeping the cigarette situation from

Lauren even a minute longer, maybe the talk could keep until tomorrow as well. She'd be in a better frame of mind—less likely to lock Max in his room and throw away the key.

"I agree. You need to take care of Emma tonight, and I need to take care of some business." He pulled into her driveway and killed the engine. "I'll carry Emma into the house for you."

"Thanks, but I can get her. Max, grab my purse, please."

Caleb walked them to the door. "I'll call tomorrow, see how Emma's doing. Find out what time you want me over for supper." He gave her arm a gentle squeeze. "She'll be fine. She's already sleeping, and the pain medicine will make sure she sleeps comfortably."

Lauren looked up at him with something that resembled a smile. "I know. Thanks again, for everything. See you tomorrow."

"Count on it." He ruffled Max's hair, earning a frown from the boy. "You help your mother tonight. She'll need it."

Max gnawed on the inside of his cheek and gave a curt nod.

Walking away when he wanted to wrap his arms around all three of them was no easy feat. But Lauren would have her hands full tonight, and Caleb needed some time to think. He was in way over his head, and he knew it.

He took the scenic route through town so he could drive past Hutch's Diner. Caleb didn't know why he tortured himself. Maybe it was the vision of his mother in her polyester pink uniform, bringing him a chocolate malted topped with a mountain of whipped cream while he did his homework to the strains of Guns N' Roses, Stone Temple Pilots, and Nirvana.

Caleb found himself turning into the parking lot and pulling into the spot that Hutch had declared reserved only for Rosalee. Caleb had loved Hutch as a kid, following him around like an eager puppy, helping out in the kitchen, living on cheeseburgers and the best fries in town.

Until the day he'd come home early from school and caught his mother and Hutch having sex in his parents' bed.

Someone rapped on the driver's side window, snapping Caleb from his musings. He glanced up and was transported twenty years back in time. Hutch stood beside his truck, hands in his pockets, looking...weary. His graying, near-black hair was now completely silver, he'd lost weight, and his face seemed drawn. He looked like...an old man. A sad old man. Caleb rolled his window down.

"Heard you'd stayed in town," Hutch said.

Caleb nodded. He stared out the windshield for a moment, then swallowed his pride and met the older man's gaze. "Thinking about staying permanently."

"Your mother'd be happy."

A reluctant grin touched Caleb's mouth. Hutch Hutchinson, man of few words. "Hope so. Listen, can we talk? There are a few things I think are long overdue to be said."

Hutch nodded and took a step back. "I'll go pour us some coffee."

As soon as Caleb walked through the front door of the diner, he felt his mother's presence everywhere. The diner had about ten customers, and he smiled when a waitress walked by carrying a cheeseburger plate piled high with French fries. Caleb's stomach rumbled. He hadn't had a thing to eat since his breakfast. He strode up to the counter and slid onto a stool. The aroma of Hutch's fresh-brewed coffee was a pleasure Caleb had missed over the years. Even before he'd acquired a taste for coffee, he'd always loved the smell. Hutch set two cups down and filled them with the steaming brew.

"Can I throw you on a cheeseburger?"

"That'd be great, thanks." Caleb could almost see his mother's tearful smile as the two men she'd loved most in the world took a step toward forgiveness.

With a nod, Hutch headed into the kitchen. Caleb stirred some creamer and a little sugar into his coffee before taking a cautious sip. He smiled. Heaven in a cup. A photo scotch-taped to the wall above the cash register caught his eye. His mother stood in front of a wooden Indian, a big pair of sunglasses perched on her head, her sunburned nose crinkled in playful annoyance at whoever was taking the picture. Hutch, no doubt. They'd loved to take little road trips, and this picture smacked of Wisconsin Dells. Rosalee Hunter had had a sweet tooth a mile wide, and her favorite chocolate shop in all the Midwest was right in the heart of the Dells.

"Took that back in May. Drove down just for some fudge. She really loved that stuff."

Caleb hadn't heard Hutch walk up. The older man stared at the picture, his heart in his eyes. Caleb knew it took a lot for him to hold it together, especially in front of Caleb. Hutch had loved Rosalee very much. "I remember. Drove her there a time or two myself."

Hutch swiped his nose with his knuckles, then picked up his coffee and took a sip. "So, you doing okay?"

"Can't complain. I'm taking the electrician's exam next Friday. It'll save me a lot of money not to have to subcontract."

"True." Hutch cleared his throat, drummed his fingers on the counter. He obviously wanted to say something, but probably couldn't find the right words.

Caleb was having the same problem.

"I'd better go flip your burger."

Caleb heard the hiss and pop of the deep fryer as Hutch lowered the fries into the hot oil. He returned a minute later. "Four minutes."

"It's been a long time. I've missed those fries."

"I know."

"The cheeseburgers, too," Caleb added. "Best in Redemption."

"Best in the state," Hutch corrected with just the slightest trace of a grin.

"No arguments here."

"I loved her, you know."

Caleb's pulse quickened. He suddenly felt fourteen again. "She loved you, too."

Hutch gave a curt nod. Their gazes locked. Caleb knew it was time. Time to say what should've been said while his mother was still alive. "I can't even begin to tell you how sorry I am. I acted like an immature fool—"

"You acted like anyone your age would've, and with good reason. Though the fish heads hidden in my storage room were a bit much. Took us weeks to figure out what stunk so bad." A huge grin split the older man's face.

Caleb chuckled. "I was too young to kick your ass. It seemed like the best alternative."

"Your mother laughed herself sick over that one."

A young waitress who couldn't have been more than twenty walked up and set a steaming plate in front of Caleb. Man, he couldn't even count how many dreams he'd had over the past couple of decades featuring this big ol' plate of paradise.

"Thanks." He reached for the bottle of ketchup, squirted a pile next to the fries, and dipped one in. "Mmm, even better than I remembered." He took a huge bite of his cheeseburger next, and it was like a religious experience.

"Is it true you've been seeing Lauren Frazier?"

Caleb nearly choked on his food. He swallowed and shook his head with a reluctant chuckle. "I swear, it never ceases to amaze me how fast gossip travels in this town."

"So it's true?"

"We've...become friends. Why? Is this a problem?"

"Course not. Your mother adored Lauren and those kids."

"I heard. They didn't know Mom had passed."

Hutch took a sip of his coffee. "They haven't been in for a while, and your mom...it was sudden. No warning."

Caleb dropped his eyes to his plate. "I know." He blew out a hard breath. "I'd been planning to come up soon. Wish I'd let her know, maybe—"

"Son, don't even say it. You're not psychic. Your mother knew you loved her, and that's what matters."

Caleb met the older man's gaze. "Thanks, Hutch."

He waved it off. "Hurry up and finish your food. I have a couple of steps I need you to replace for me."

"Yes, sir." Caleb took another bite of his cheeseburger, his heart lighter than it'd been in years.

Chapter Seven

"So, are you taking the kids to the fair?"

Lauren gave Mrs. Langhart's silver bob one last squirt of hairspray, and then handed her a mirror. "I have plans tonight, so maybe tomorrow. I might let Max go for a couple hours later with his friends."

Mrs. Langhart held the mirror up and examined Lauren's work from every angle twice over. Lauren resisted the urge to roll her eyes.

"Make sure you pat him down before you let him out the door."

"Pardon me?"

The older woman glanced furtively around, then lowered her voice to a conspiratorial whisper. "Max and those hoodlum friends of his left a bunch of butts on the sidewalk in front of my house."

Lauren froze. "Are you saying Max has been smoking?"

"That's exactly what I'm saying. They're like little sailors out there, smoking and cussing. Larry had to shoo them away just the other night."

No fricken way. It couldn't be true. Max was only ten years old, for God's sake, a little boy. Then Lauren remembered Caleb had found a cigarette butt in the backyard, and her heart constricted. "Mrs. Langhart, I am so sorry. I had no idea any of this was going on. I appreciate you bringing it to my attention."

Mrs. Langhart gave Lauren's hand a pat. "You have your hands full with that one, my dear. Maybe the handsome carpenter you've been dating can help keep that boy of yours in line."

"Oh, we're not dating. Caleb was kind enough to make some minor repairs in exchange for a few home-cooked meals."

"Uh-huh," the older woman said with a knowing smirk. "Well, your Caleb is quite a looker. And take it from me, honey, he's not coming around for your cooking, as delicious as it no doubt is."

Lauren's cheeks grew hot. She resisted the urge to reach up and feel them.

Mrs. Langhart climbed off the chair and retrieved her wallet from her purse. "Here." She stuffed some money into Lauren's hand and folded her fingers around it. "Take this and buy yourself a new pair of high heels. Nothing like a sexy pair of shoes to give a man ideas." She winked at Lauren, grasped her purse, and slipped out the front door.

Lauren blew out a hard breath as she stuffed the money in her pocket. Max smoking. Never in a million years would she have guessed that. My God, she felt like the worst mother in the world. How could she be so clueless about something so important?

She got up and filled her coffee cup, then picked up the cordless and paced back and forth across the linoleum, her mind a jumbled mess of questions and concerns. Max was at Caleb's place helping him stain boards for a fencing job, and the two of them planned to head back around four for supper. She stared at the phone, tempted to call Caleb and have him drag Max's little smoking ass home so Lauren could ground him till he turned thirty.

With a heavy-hearted sigh, she set the phone down and resumed her pacing. Emma was lying on the couch watching cartoons, a little sleepy from her pain medication. Lauren changed the bandages and put ointment on her tender little fingers. Now that she knew Max was most likely responsible, Lauren wanted to scream, she wanted to cry—she wanted to hunt John Frazier down so she could string him up by his balls from the nearest tree.

The phone rang in her hand. Lauren jumped a foot, her heart pounding like a jackhammer. Good God, woman, get a grip. She took a deep breath, eye-rolled herself and picked up on the fifth ring. "Hello?"

"Hey, pretty lady, we still on for four?"

Caleb. "Sure are. So, how's it going? Max behaving himself?"

"Yep. Working his heart out, in fact. I may have myself an apprentice in a few years. If it's okay with you, that is," he promptly added.

Lauren dropped onto a chair and closed her eyes. Caleb was so good for Max. Part of her was scared to death that if things didn't work out between her and Caleb, Max would take it twice as hard as when his father left.

Lauren nibbled on her bottom lip. Or maybe she was the one who'd take it twice as hard. Her marriage had been over for months by the time John had taken off for deeper cleavagedpastures, so if not for the devastative heartbreak his disappearance had caused their children, she'd have gassed up the car for him personally. Caleb, however, she wasn't ready to let go of yet. "I think that'd be great. He can even help out on weekends once school is back in session. Keep his butt out of trouble," she added in a mutter.

"Excellent idea. We'll see you in a few hours."

Lauren hung up just as someone knocked on the door. Later she'd worry about how to confront Mr. Ashtray Breath. Right now, she had to give Mrs. Dilliard a perm and pray the old girl didn't try to pull her rods out again.

Caleb set the phone in its cradle and returned to the garage where Max was already making record time on his newest section of fencing.

He gave the kid a pat on the back. "Max, if it wasn't against the law, I'd have you working eight-hour shifts with me."

"I could handle it. I'm strong for my age."

Caleb's chest tightened at Max's eager response. He was a great kid, and his father was either the most selfish bastard in the world or the dumbest. Any man should be proud to have this kid as their son. He was hardworking, intelligent, caring. He just needed some guidance, which Caleb was more than willing to give. Only one problem. Caleb had no idea what the future held for him and Lauren. He was crazy about her. Drawn to her like he'd never been any other woman. He wanted her in his life...and in his bed. Caleb gave his head a rueful shake. They hadn't even shared a kiss yet, for crissakes.

But even if things didn't work out between them, maybe she'd allow Max and him to remain friends.

"No doubt about it. You nearly blew my mind when you lifted that section up by yourself."

Max paused with the paintbrush in his hand and looked up at Caleb as if he'd just paid him the mother of all compliments. "I could do the most pushups and chin-ups in my class last year. Won a trophy and everything."

Caleb smiled. "Don't surprise me a bit. Tall as you are, you're probably the fastest runner, too."

Max puffed up his chest. "Yep. Even faster than Lori Switzer, and she's fast for a girl."

"I bet she is." Caleb's smile turned into an ear-to-ear grin. "You ready for a root beer?"

"Sure. Just gotta finish this last board."

Caleb grabbed two cans from the fridge and held one out to Max, who looked suddenly thoughtful as he stared at his paintbrush.

"Are you gonna tell on me for the cigarettes?"

Caleb met Max's gaze as he reached out for the soda. "I don't think it's right for me to keep something this important from your mom."

"I swear, though, I'll never smoke again. I only started 'cause Eddie called me a chicken shi—well, you know. I don't even inhale."

Caleb popped the tab on his soda and took a long pull as he considered. The two of them had been building a bond, and the last thing Caleb wanted to do was break it. He wanted Max to know he could trust him, count on him. And maybe, he rationalized, Lauren was better off not knowing. Max was her little boy, no matter how big he was, and Caleb knew how hard she'd take the news that her ten-year-old boy had been smoking. Because one thing he'd learned in the short time he'd known her— Lauren was an amazing mother. "I won't tell your mom, but you've got to swear to me you'll never touch another cigarette as long as you live."

Max's paintbrush stopped moving again. He frowned. "You mean until I'm an adult, right? I can do what I want when I turn eighteen."

Arms crossed over his chest, Caleb shook his head. The little stinker. "I mean ever. So promise right now or I'll have no choice but to tell your mother."

Max's mouth dropped open in disbelief. "Hey, that's totally unfair. I'm supposed to be able to do what I want when I'm an adult."

With a disbelieving raise of an eyebrow, Caleb leaned one hip against the wall. "So you're telling me you can rob a bank if you feel like it just because you're an adult? Or you can park your car in the middle of the street and hold up traffic just because you're an adult? You can cut in line at the grocery store, just because you're an adult? Wish somebody had told me that one."

Max rolled his eyes. "That's just stupid."

"So is smoking." Caleb had to hold back a grin as Max heaved a resigned sigh.

"Fine, I promise. I'll never smoke again. Happy?"

"Delirious. Now, you ready for your next section?"

Lauren watched a laughing Max and Caleb stroll through the door with mixed emotions. They obviously enjoyed each other's company, and as Caleb gave Max a pat on the back, her son looked up at him as if he'd hung the moon. Tears stung her eyes and she quickly blinked them away.

She loved that Max had a male figure he could talk to and look up to. Even if things didn't progress between her and Caleb, Max could still work with him on the weekends and during the summer. If Max kept himself busy working with Caleb, he wouldn't be running around with his punk friends, smoking, cussing, and Lord knew what else.

But what if Caleb decided to head back to Chicago, his home for the past thirteen years?

"Mom, we got more than half the boards stained! Caleb said I work a paintbrush faster'n anyone he's ever seen!"

"It's true, the kid's something else."

Yeah, he's something else all right. Disappointment burned in her gut when she recalled her earlier conversation with Mrs. Langhart. "Thank you for taking him under your wing." Without making eye contact with either one of them, Lauren strode into the kitchen to check on her lasagna. "Max, please go wash your hands for supper. It's almost ready."

She heard the thud of Caleb's work boots as he came up behind her. She flinched when his hands settled on her shoulders.

"Something wrong?"

"No, I'm sorry. I was just thinking about something, and you startled me."

He dropped his hands, and she turned to face him, plastering on as big a smile as she could muster.

"Man, that's the fakest smile I've ever seen. Come on, tell me what's got you so jumpy."

She moved around the counter to dig her bread knife out of the drawer. "I got some disturbing news today, and I'm just...I don't know what the heck to do about it."

Caleb flipped one of her chairs around and straddled it. "You wanna tell me? Maybe I can help."

"I hope you can," she admitted. She sliced the loaf of Italian bread in half lengthwise and starting smearing it with a generous layer of garlic spread. "I found out today…" She looked up and met his gaze. "Max has been smoking."

Caleb didn't so much as bat an eye. Lauren dropped the knife on the counter and gawked at him. "You knew?"

"Yeah, I did."

"Well, when the hell were you going to tell me? My God, Caleb, Emma burned her fingers on a lit cigarette. Max's lit cigarette."

He cast a quick glance over his shoulder. "Look, I'd planned on telling you, but Max begged me not to. Swore he'd never light up again for as long as he lived if I didn't tell you. I thought the boy deserved that much. He's been through a lot this past year, needed someone he could trust."

Ouch. Though she knew Caleb hadn't meant to imply that her son didn't trust her—even if she knew that was exactly the case—hearing the words aloud was like an arrow to the heart.

"And the cigarette Emma picked up wasn't Max's, it was some punk friend of his who snuck into the backyard while we were talking. He flicked the burning butt in the grass, and Emma picked it up before Max could get to it. The kid split as soon as she started crying."

Lauren chewed on the inside of her cheek, at least somewhat relieved Max hadn't been smoking the cigarette that burned his sister. "Caleb, I'm grateful you've taken such an interest in Max. You've made more progress with him in a week than I have in over a year. But you should've told me and let me decide what to do."

Before Caleb could respond, Max zipped down the stairs and flew into the kitchen, an almost smug smile on his face. "Are we gonna work again tomorrow? I bet we can finish the rest by noon if we start at seven."

Despite everything, Lauren laughed. "In the morning?" Max hadn't dragged his butt out of bed before ten a.m. since summer break began.

Max surprised her with a sheepish grin. "I could do it if I set my alarm clock. Can I, Mom?"

"Max, tomorrow's Saturday. Most people don't work on the weekends."

"Actually," Caleb laced his fingers over the back of the chair, "I'd love to get the boards finished tomorrow. Then I could start putting the fence up on Monday."

Lauren eyed Caleb, more torn than she'd been in a long time. Max deserved to be grounded for a month, not allowed to go out and have fun. Only the "fun" was hard, honest work, and the fact that he was willing—heck, had even suggested—to get up early to do so, was enough incentive to agree. "Fine. But when that alarm goes off, I don't want to hear any whining. This was your idea, so you won't disappoint Caleb."

DONNA MARIE ROGERS

"No way, I swear. I really like staining. And I'm good at it. You know I'm not good at a lot of stuff."

She clucked her tongue. "That's not true. You've just never really applied yourself before. And you were getting pretty good at the guitar until you quit." She set the bread, garlic side up, on a foil-lined pan.

"I was thinking about taking lessons again. I mean, if you'll let me."

Lauren spun around, surprised. "Of course, I'll let you. You know how disappointed I was when you wanted to quit."

"But can we afford it? If not, I can pay for it out of my own money."

"Max, I appreciate the offer, but you'll put your money in the bank. I'll pay for your lessons."

"Hey," Caleb said, "why don't you play me something while we're waiting on supper? I always wanted to learn how to play guitar."

Max jumped up so fast Caleb and Lauren both laughed. Lauren said, "Peek in on your sister, would you? She's awfully quiet, and her movie should be about over by now."

"'Kay." Max took off like a shot.

"He's eager to please you," she told him, unsure of how that made her feel. Caleb seemed to be a great guy—not to mention sexy as a box of Godiva chocolates—but really, she'd known the man less than a week. Maybe things were moving along a little too fast…hell, who was she kidding? Things were absolutely moving too fast. For all she knew, Caleb could pack up and skip town tomorrow, and where would that leave them? Emma was young and would quickly forget about him. But Max? It would kill Lauren to watch her son withdraw into his angry shell again—maybe for good this time.

"He's eager to please period. And I really do love his company. The kid has a great sense of humor, believe it or not."

Lauren's hand stilled. "He hasn't told you any dirty jokes, has he?"

Caleb laughed. "Why in the world would you ask me that?"

Her lips twitched. "Just checking."

"Relax, he hasn't told me a single limerick. It's just when he's telling me something, he's so dry and witty. Kinda reminds me of Hutch a little."

"Not surprising. Max idolizes Hutch. I need to take the kids to see him soon. Tell him how sorry we are about Rosalee…your mother. Wow, that still boggles my mind."

"You'll never know how much it means to me that you all knew and liked my mom."

Lauren's heart melted a tiny bit more. "We more than liked her. We absolutely adored her. You come from good stock, Mr. Hunter."

Lauren checked the lasagna—light golden brown and bubbly. She carefully pulled it from the oven and set it on the counter to cool for a few minutes, cranked the oven up to 425° and slid in her garlic bread.

Caleb stood and came around to look at the lasagna, his expression priceless. "Man, if there was an award for the most perfect supper, this would win, hands down."

Lauren nearly twittered, but caught herself. Sheesh, what was it about this man that turned her brain to mush? Turned her from a strong, independent woman into a simpering fool? "Thanks. Hope it tastes as good as it looks."

"No doubt in my mind."

Max came skipping down the stairs, guitar in hand. When he saw that supper was about ready, his face fell. "Guess there's no time to play."

"We must have time for one song." Caleb directed a questioning look her way.

"Just one."

"Awesome." Max sat down and got comfortable. He strummed the guitar, tuned a string, then started playing.

Chapter Eight

Caleb watched in amazement as Max's fingers expertly moved over the strings and out came an old Rolling Stones classic, "Paint It Black". Man, the kid played like a pro!

"I told you he's good," Lauren excitedly whispered, pride in her son making her even more beautiful.

"You certainly didn't exaggerate. So, the Rolling Stones, hey? Isn't he a bit young to know their music?"

"His instructor is a hippie, straight out of Woodstock. All the songs he's taught Max are from the sixties and seventies."

"Then I look forward to hearing every song he knows."

As soon as Max strummed the last note, Caleb and Lauren clapped like crazy.

"Crap, I forgot about the garlic bread!" Lauren exclaimed. She ran over and blew out a sigh of relief as she pulled the pan from the oven. "Perfect."

"Smells awesome," Caleb said. "Man, am I starving."

"Me, too!" Max chimed in. "My mom makes the best lasagna in the world. She can cook anything, right, Mom?"

Lauren gazed at Max with a bemused smile. "Well, I draw the line at octopus and insects, but besides that, I'll give anything a try."

"Two things I can guarantee I'll never ask you to cook." Caleb promised with a wink. "What can I do to help?"

"You can carry the lasagna to the table." She handed him two oven mitts. "Max, please go get your sister. And be careful of her hand."

Caleb looked up in time to see a wave of guilt pass over Max's face. Poor kid still felt responsible for what happened to Emma.

Ten minutes later, they all sat down to their first meal as a family. Caleb nearly choked on the thought. Beads of cold sweat broke out on his forehead. Family? He eyed each one of them and, disconcertingly, found them all smiling back at him. Clearing his throat and pushing his reservations aside, Caleb dropped his gaze to his plate and forked in a bite of lasagna. His taste buds did a happy dance. Damn, the woman could cook. He looked up again to find Emma grinning from ear to ear.

"Yummy, Ca'yib?"

He met Lauren's gaze for a brief second and a strange undercurrent passed between them. He wanted to kiss her so bad he could taste her. Get a grip, Hunter. "Delicious, punkin."

By the time Lauren served the apple pie a la mode, Caleb thought he would burst. "You guys don't honestly eat this good all the time, do you?"

"No, but we can. I mean, if you want to. Right, Mom?" Max looked so earnest and hopeful, Caleb wanted to assure the boy he wasn't going anywhere. But how could he make such a promise when Caleb had no idea where any of this would lead? Realistically, he was a virtual stranger to them.

And he hadn't even kissed the woman yet. That was the problem. So much depended upon something as simple as a kiss. If the kiss had no magic, if they broke apart without so much as a tingle, that was the end of it.

Though, somehow, Caleb doubted that would be the case.

Max stood up as soon as he'd scarfed down his pie. "Hey, can we go rent a movie?"

He carried his plate and fork to the sink and even rinsed them. Lauren raised a brow, her expression bemused. Caleb got the feeling Max didn't put his dirty dishes in the sink all too often. "I'm game. It's only a little after five."

"Sounds great," Lauren chimed in. "Can we make a quick stop? I'd really like to stop at the diner and say hi to Hutch."

"Me, too! I can tell him I'm gonna start taking guitar lessons again."

The strangest sense of panic tightened Caleb's chest. Ignoring it, he said, "It's already after five. I'm sure he must've headed home by now."

"Nuh-uh. He stays till seven on Fridays 'cause the bowling league lets out, and they all head over for burgers."

"Maybe we shouldn't stay out too long, though, with Emma's hand and all."

"I go store, too! Me, too, Ca'yib!"

Caleb let out a silent, frustrated breath, but Lauren must have caught it because her gaze grew pensive. "If you don't want to stop, we don't have to. I'll take the kids into town tomorrow."

"Mom, the diner'll be closed tomorrow 'cause of the fair," Max reminded her. "We have to go tonight."

Jesus, what was the matter with him? So what if Hutch would wink and tease. So what if the rumors swirling around town reached Twitter speed. He was a grown man, and grown men dated. Sometimes they dated women with kids. A ready-made family. Nothing wrong with that. Nothing at all.

"Hey, you look like you're gonna puke," Max informed him. "Want me to get you a bucket?"

Caleb shook off his funk and managed a smile. "Thanks, but I'm fine. Just remembered something I forgot to order for a job coming up this week. Do me a favor and remind me about it tomorrow."

"'Kay. So, are we going to the diner and video store, or what?"

"Me go, too!" Emma insisted.

Lauren cast him an uncertain smile, putting all his nagging doubts to rest...for the time being, anyway. "Let's go. Last one to my truck has to kiss Hutch."

"Now, this is a sight I like to see," Hutch said as they entered the diner a short time later and strode forward to greet him. Lauren adjusted

Emma on her hip, then leaned in and gave him a kiss on his adorably scruffy cheek. Hutch turned red as a lobster. "What was that for?"

She grinned. "I forgot my purse."

He cocked a bushy brow. "If you want me to start a tab for you..."

Lauren laughed. "No, it's just I was the last one...never mind. We're on our way to rent a movie, but wanted to stop in and say hello. It's been way too long." She reached out and touched his arm. "I'm so sorry about Rosalee. She'll be missed."

The older man gave a curt nod. "Thanks."

"Hey, Hutch." Max hopped up on a stool. "I decided to start taking guitar lessons again, so you're gonna be seeing us more often very soon."

"Glad to hear it." He gave Max a pat on the head.

"Can I get you guys anything?"

Caleb pretended to consider, sending her a teasing grin. All Lauren could think about was how badly she wanted to kiss him. She'd been dreaming about it all week long. So far, she'd fantasized about kissing him in her barber's chair, in the swing out back, in his truck, her car, the movie theater, under the stars, in the rain. Her pulse kicked up, sending tingles of awareness to every nerve in her body. She was suddenly very glad to be wearing her padded bra.

"Actually, Lauren just made the best Italian meal I've ever had, complete with apple pie a la mode."

"Lucky you." Hutch's eyes crinkled at the corners, his lips curving just the slightest bit.

"Sucka! Sucka!" Emma shouted, pointing toward a plastic jar filled with Dum Dum pops on the counter.

Hutch unscrewed the lid and held the jar aloft. "Go ahead, sweetheart, pick any one you want."

She reached in and managed to grab three. She grinned up at Hutch, who then held the jar out for Max. Max fished around until he'd found the last root beer sucker.

When Hutch started to twist the lid back on, Caleb teased, "Hey, what about me?"

Lauren laughed as Hutch extended his arm and gave the jar a shake.

Max rolled his eyes. "The suckers are for the kids, not adults," he informed Caleb.

"I'll have you know I've been pulling candy out of this jar since I was your age, probably before. And trust me, you're never too old for candy. Right, Hutch?" Caleb leaned over and reached under the counter. He pulled out a bag of M&Ms with a flourish.

"Hey, now." Hutch's brow beetled into a mock frown. "That's my secret stash, boy. Ain't nothin' sacred?"

Lauren laughed while Caleb held the bag just out of the older man's reach.

"Since I'm too old to jump up and grab 'em, guess I'll have to put you on my no-service list." He pretended to write on his order tablet. "No more cheeseburgers for Caleb."

Caleb chuckled, and Lauren's heart swelled as she witnessed the affection these two men had for each other. Since legend had it that Hutch and Rosalee had been together for decades, Caleb and Hutch must have been very close. Maybe like father and son since, from the impression Caleb had left, his own father had left him when he was still a kid.

Caleb handed over the M&Ms with a wink. "Come on, gang, we'd better get to the video store before they rent out all the movies."

"Like that could really happen," Max said with a roll of his eyes.

"Hey, you never know. What if everyone in town decided to head to the video store at the exact same time?" Caleb grinned, ruffled Max's hair, and escorted them out of the diner as everyone waved and Emma blew kisses to Hutch.

It was just past six by the time they arrived back home, and Lauren realized she was looking forward to this as much as Max. Maybe more. She popped a couple of bags of microwave popcorn, poured them all a glass of soda—except Emma, who got watered-down apple juice—and they settled on the couch to watch the movie. Max and Emma both insisted on sitting next to Caleb, so Lauren curled up in the corner and enjoyed her space.

Emma fell asleep about halfway through the movie. Lauren gently lifted her from Caleb's lap and carried her upstairs. She wanted to change her bandage, but hated to wake her, so she decided to wait until morning and headed back downstairs. By the time the credits were rolling, Max hadn't so much as yawned, and Lauren was kicking herself for giving him soda. Darn it, she wanted some alone time with Caleb.

She wanted the kiss she'd been craving since the moment she'd laid eyes on him.

"Wanna play Monopoly?" Max jumped off the couch and started rummaging around in the hall closet. "Or we could play Sorry!, that's another good one."

"Sorry!" Lauren and Caleb said at the same time.

They glanced at each other and laughed. Max shook his head, no doubt figuring all adults were nuts. He pulled the game out and shut the closet door. "Come on," he ordered as he carried the game into the kitchen. "I'll set it up. And dibs on blue."

"Green!" Caleb called out. He lowered his voice to barely a whisper. "What are the chances he'll pass out before I have to leave?"

"I'll take yellow, Max!" She shrugged and grinned up at him. "Pretty much slim to none, I'm thinking. Why? Got any ideas?"

He scooched over and ran one finger up her bare arm, to her equally bare shoulder, sending a delicious chill to all her pleasure points. He trailed it up her collarbone to her throat, ending at the tender spot just below her ear. "I've got a few."

Lauren shivered in response.

"Come on, you two, let's go!"

Caleb winked at her, then stood up and helped her to her feet.

Right after the third game, Caleb made a big show of looking at the clock and widening his eyes as if in astonishment. Lauren barely repressed a giggle. "Holy cow, ten-thirty? Max, if you plan to start working at seven, you'd better get your butt up to bed."

"But I'm not even tired," he complained.

"Hey, kid, it was your idea to work tomorrow," Caleb reminded him. "I don't plan to get up early for nothing. If you don't get to bed now, you'll never drag your bones out of bed by six-thirty. And I plan to pick you up around ten-to."

"He's right, honey." Lauren started putting the game pieces back in the box. "Besides, as soon as your head hits the pillow, you'll be tired. Trust me."

Max heaved a comically dramatic sigh. "Fine." He got up and dragged his feet toward the stairs. He'd taken maybe four steps before turning. "Can we stop at Coffee To Chai For in the morning for sweet rolls? I'll pay for 'em."

"Sounds like a plan. But I'll buy since it's the boss's job to feed his employees, not the other way around."

"Cool. 'Night." Max returned the game to the closet and headed upstairs.

As soon as they heard his bedroom door close, Caleb got up and strode around the table, his eyes brimming with mischief. He held out his hand, and Lauren took it without a moment's hesitation. He gave her a gentle tug, and when she rose to her feet, he kissed her knuckles before taking her into his arms.

"I think this moment has waited long enough, don't you?"

Chapter Nine

Caleb cupped the side of her face, his thumb tracing along her cheekbone as he leaned in and gently pressed his lips to hers. It was a chaste kiss, all too brief, and Lauren barely held back a whimper of frustration. Had he decided he'd had enough from just that small sampling? Had there been no spark on his end? Because, good God, the man had practically melted the mascara from her eyelashes with just that one simple kiss. Her heart pounded furiously against her ribs as she waited for his next move.

He pulled back slightly and met her gaze, almost as if gauging her reaction. Then he leaned back in and reclaimed her mouth—this time with ravenous need. Finally, the kiss she'd been craving all week!

Lauren wrapped her arms around his neck and held on for dear life as he slanted his mouth across hers and proceeded to kiss her breathless. His lips were soft and coaxing, yet firm and demanding as they worked their magic, sending needles of pleasure to every nerve in her body.

Caleb maneuvered them so he could sit down on one of the chairs and pull her onto his lap, never breaking the kiss. Lauren met the rasp of his tongue stroke for stroke, caressing the nape of his neck, tunneling her fingers through his thick, baby-soft curls. She couldn't remember ever being this turned on before, this into a kiss. Holy fricken wow, talk about worth the wait!

She moaned, leaning into him, dissolving into his heat, pulse roaring in her ears. Lauren turned in his arms, bringing her leg around so she could straddle his lap and snuggle even closer, plastering herself against his broad, hard chest. Caleb answered her silent plea with a growl of his own, crushing her in his arms, his hands caressing a fiery trail down her back, cupping her butt in his big hands. Their mouths meshed with escalating hunger, their tongues moving in a dance as old as time, both giving as much as they took. Lauren felt sure she would drown in the heady sensations coursing through her.

The proof of his desire was nestled between them, and it took all her self-control not to move against him. It had been so long since—

Caleb tore his lips from hers and rested his forehead against hers, his breath coming out in ragged pants.

"Wha—?" Lauren could barely draw air into her lungs to speak. "Is something wrong?" she finally managed to whisper.

"I think Emma woke up," he whispered right back.

Lauren pulled back in alarm and shot a look toward the stairs. How could she have not heard her? "I'll be right back," she murmured, unable to meet his gaze. She climbed off his lap with as much dignity as possible and raced up the stairs.

Emma had indeed woken up, but Lauren rubbed her back for a few minutes, and she fell right back to sleep. She stuck her head in the bathroom on her way back to check her face in the mirror, make sure the words "bad mother" weren't etched into her forehead.

Caleb stood as soon as she entered the kitchen. "Is she all right? It wasn't her hand, was it?"

"No, just fussing. She fell right back to sleep." Lauren wrapped her arms around herself and walked past him to the sink for a glass of water.

Caleb came up behind her, but didn't touch her. "Is something wrong?"

She took a sip, then another, too embarrassed to turn around and face him. "I didn't even hear her. What does that say about my maternal instinct?"

He frowned and took her in his arms. "You're a wonderful mother, Lauren. You got wrapped up in the moment, which, to be honest, is a pretty big compliment."

She gazed up at him, hoping her heart wasn't in her eyes. "But you heard her. Does that mean you weren't as...that it didn't affect you the same way...?"

He silenced her with a quick kiss. "Shh. All it means is I'm a military man who's attuned to the sounds around him. The kiss knocked my socks off, lady."

A hopeful smile tugged at her lips. "Really? Well...good."

Caleb chuckled softly. He reached up and cupped the back of her head, as if ready to prove his point, but then dropped his hands with obvious regret. "If I don't leave now..."

"You won't be able to leave at all?"

He kissed her on the forehead and took a step back. "Exactly."

Lauren realized, as she walked him to the door, they'd never discussed the fair. "Any chance you'd like to join the kids and me Saturday for a stroll through the fair?"

"Every chance. I'd love to, thanks. And it'll be my treat. We'll consider it a first date."

"No arguments from the financially challenged," she teased. "Although please don't think you have to."

"I want to." He smiled, his eyes crinkling as he gazed down at her. He tipped her chin up and gave her one last kiss before walking out the door.

Holy…Wow. Lauren closed the door behind him and collapsed against it, her knees ridiculously weak, her heart pumping fast. Every inch of her crackled with sexual frustration. Never had she felt such…raw desire before, such a powerful physical need. She wanted him. Lord, how she wanted him.

Maybe she'd take Mrs. Langhart's advice and buy herself a sexy new pair of heels tomorrow. And maybe she'd see if Carrie was available to babysit for a few hours.

"At this rate, we'll be done by eleven," Caleb told Max the next morning as they took a quick break to wolf down a couple of sweet rolls.

"Cool. I'll be able to meet Eddie and Pete right when the fair opens at noon." Max grabbed a second apple fritter and stuffed it in his mouth.

Caleb gave his head an amused shake. The kid could down a sweet roll faster than he could. And Caleb was no slouch in the eating department. "You're not planning on meeting up with Bucky, are you?" Caleb took a nonchalant bite of his chocolate-covered long john.

Max looked up, a frown creasing his forehead, the apple fritter forgotten. "No. I never want to see that asshole again."

Caleb's brows drew together. "Hope you don't use words like that around your mother."

Max had the audacity to grin. "Heck, no. She'd put a drop of hot sauce on my lips while I was sleeping."

Caleb chuckled, easily imagining Lauren doing just that. "Sounds like her. But for the record, no swearing around me either, all right?"

Max gave a quick, sullen nod. "Sure. Hey, what about jerk off? Can I say that?"

Caleb grinned, despite himself. God, he loved this kid. "Negative, pal."

They polished off their midmorning snack, and got back to work staining the boards. They finished by ten after eleven, much to Max's delight. And when Caleb handed him fifty bucks, he stared at the money in open-mouthed shock.

"I appreciate hard work, so that's a bonus for working your tail off. I plan to give your mom what I owe you to stick in the bank, but the extra is just between us, got it? For the fair today."

"Got it! Thanks!"

"And hey, I'm planning to take you, your mom, and Emma to the fair tomorrow for a few hours, if that's all right…?"

"That would awesome! The fireworks are tomorrow night. Can we stay for 'em?"

"Absolutely. No way I'd want to miss the fireworks."

He dropped Max off at home, and since Lauren was in the middle of a hair appointment, he told her to give him a call later. Caleb had a few stops to make, including a couple of service calls, and giving an estimate on a kitchen remodel. He stopped at Hutch's for a cheeseburger, visiting with the old man for a while before heading home. After a quick shower, he settled in to study for the electrician exam.

As he strode through the house, book in hand, a nagging doubt crept into his mind. He tried to shake it off, but suddenly found himself full of uncertainties. A ready-made family...was he crazy to even consider it? He'd never expected to fall so hard and fast for anyone, let alone a woman with two kids—one with major anger issues thanks to a father who, in Caleb's opinion, should be sitting in a jail cell for abandoning his children.

Caleb slapped the book on the kitchen table and plopped down on a chair. Doubt and confusion warred within him until he thought his brain might explode. He was simply over-thinking it, that's all. He'd known Lauren and the kids less than a week, for crying out loud. Nothing to get worked up over. He hadn't even decided for sure if he wanted to stay in Redemption.

The doorbell rang. Caleb blew out a hard breath, loath to answer it. He wasn't exactly in a mood for company. With reluctance, he shoved back from the table and headed for the front door.

Standing on Caleb's front porch in nothing but a mid-thigh length black trench coat and a pair of red stilettos, Lauren immediately second-guessed her ridiculous plan the moment her finger pressed the doorbell. Crap…maybe if she hurried she could get the hell out of there before—

The door swung open and there stood Caleb, his expression priceless as he took her in from coifed head to painted toe. "Am I dreaming?" he teased, leaning back against the doorjamb with his arms crossed.

"Yes. Yes, you are. Now close the door and go back to sleep." Good Lord, the man was gorgeous in his snug-fitting white T-shirt tucked into a pair of well-worn Levi's. Barefoot and freshly showered, with his tousled hair slightly damp and smelling of masculine spice, she swore he could have stepped right off the cover of a magazine.

Taking her all in, he gave his head a shake, as if he couldn't quite believe his eyes. "I have to admit, you…dressed like this, was the last thing I expected to find on my doorstep."

Her face flamed. "Seriously, what do you say I jump back in my car and race home, and you pretend you didn't just witness my total humiliation?"

Caleb straightened. "Not a chance." He grabbed her by the hand, hauled her inside, and promptly shut the door. "So…what brings you by?"

Somehow he managed to ask the question with a straight face, the shit. "Avon calling."

At that he laughed. He reached out and fingered the collar of her coat, which she had clutched in a tight fist. "I've never had a woman stop by to seduce me before."

"I suppose that's good to know." Christ, just grow a pair already and do what you came here to do.

"You completely naked under that coat?"

He looked about ready to rip it open and find out for himself. The thought sent all her pink parts into overdrive. She caught her bottom lip between her teeth and struck what she hoped was a sexy pose. "May-be."

"What do I have to do to find out?"

"To be honest, a drink might help. Got any wine?"

He thought about it for a moment, then grasped her hand and led her into the kitchen. He opened the fridge, pulled out an unopened bottle of white wine and handed it to her, then grabbed two glasses from the cabinet above the sink and a corkscrew from the drawer below it. Without a word, he led her down the hall to the third room on the left. A bedroom.

"Yours?" she asked as she looked around with interest. The room, done in shades of blue, with a beautiful pine, six-drawer side-by-side armoire and matching panel headboard was quite masculine in tone. But the room seemed to be missing the usual personal bric-a-brac you would find in someone's bedroom. Just a couple of framed prints on the walls and antique looking water bowl and pitcher set on top of the dresser.

"The guest room. I've been sleeping in here since…I returned home."

Home. Lauren's hopes soared. That he still considered Redemption home was definitely promising. "And the bed's made. I'm impressed." Great, direct his attention to the bed. Now that's all he'll be focusing on.

You came over in a thong and high heels to seduce him, dumb ass. Isn't the bed what you want him to focus on? And if his initial reaction was any indication, his mind's been focused there since the moment he opened the front door.

She delicately cleared her throat. "Is there something wrong with your own room? Or did your mom remodel it into a den or something?"

"No, it looks pretty much the same as when I left: posters all over the walls, shelves full of signed Packers paraphernalia." He grinned. "A stack of nudie mags under my bed."

Lauren rolled her eyes.

He set the glasses down on the nightstand and took the bottle from her hand. "So…who's watching the kids?"

"My neighbor, Carrie." Lauren sat down on the edge of the bed and squeezed her thighs together. Her trench coat billowed slightly. After a quick glance at Caleb, who had deftly worked the cork from the bottle, she pressed it down and crossed her ankles. Good Lord, you'd think she was a virgin the way her nerves were getting to her. Take a deep breath and relax. You want this—you want him.

Caleb handed her a glass of wine and sat down next to her. They both took a couple of sips. Lauren watched him from her peripheral vision while feigning interest in the painting over the bed. She could feel the heat of his gaze as if it were a living thing, consuming her from the inside out. Miracle she didn't burst into flames.

"I don't know what it is you do to me, lady, but I swear I'm as anxious as the first time I had a girl alone in my room."

"Really? Not me, I'm cool as a cucumber."

Caleb chuckled. "What a pair we are." He drained his glass, and then poured himself another. Guess she wasn't the only one with unsteady nerves. He gulped down half the second glass, twirled it around in his hands a few times, then finally turned to face her. "I've wanted you since the first moment I laid eyes on you." As soon as the words left his mouth, he gave his head self-deprecating shake. "Sorry. That sounded a whole lot better in my head. Talk about pathetic clichés."

"Actually, it was the most romantic thing any man has ever said to me. My ex wasn't one to waste words, and sadly, he was my first. And my only." She took another sip of her wine before casting him a sidelong glance. "Now who's pathetic?"

Caleb took her glass from her hand and set both on the floor. "You're beautiful, smart, funny…any man would be damn lucky to have you. And you deserved a helluva lot better than an asshole like that for your first." He cupped the side of her face and gently traced the hollow of her cheek with his thumb.

Lauren's eyes drifted shut as the tenderness of his touch nearly overwhelmed her. Amazed by how much she'd come to desire this man, and to trust him, she leaned into his strength, absorbing it like a dry sponge. It had been so long since she and John were intimate, but as anxious as she was right now, there really was nowhere on earth she'd rather be.

"You okay?" he murmured, his warm breath whispering over her cheek, causing goose bumps to break out across her heated skin. "If you've changed your mind, if you're not ready for this, I'll understand."

She turned slightly, just enough to meet his gaze. "No, I want this. I mean, I'm the one who..." She waved a hand at herself to make her point. "It's just been awhile, you know?"

He traced the line of her jaw, the column of her throat. "Believe it or not, it's been awhile for me, too. In fact..." His words trailed off, and he hung his head for a second. "Damn. I don't have any protection."

"I do." Her cheeks grew hot as a slow smile spread across his handsome face. "Carrie stuffed a few condoms in my hand as I was leaving."

He leaned in and kissed her, a slow drag of his lips across hers. Lauren pressed against him, eager for his touch, wanting this man so badly she was practically shaking with need. Throwing caution to the wind, she disentangled herself from his arms and stood up, ready to shed her coat—along with her inhibitions.

Caleb leaned back and held her gaze, his smile reassuring. She smiled coyly, catching her bottom lip between her teeth as she slowly unbuttoned her coat and spread it open before letting it drop to the floor. Standing before him in nothing but a pair of red stilettos and a lacy red thong, Lauren held her breath as he raked his gaze up and down her slightly trembling frame.

"My God, you're stunning," he said, rising to his feet to stand before her. Caleb drank in the sight of her, his gaze so hot it literally warmed her from head to toe. He grabbed the hem of his T-shirt and yanked it over his head, tossing it on the floor beside her coat.

Having Caleb semi naked as well helped to settle her nerves a bit, and she eagerly reached out to trace a finger over his tight abs. "You're pretty spectacular yourself."

He stepped closer and cupped both of her breasts in his big hands. Lauren's head fell back and her eyes fluttered shut as he teased and molded, her nipples tightening into pebbled peaks. A soft moan escaped her as heat flooded her core and her entire body sizzled to life.

"God, how I want you," Caleb admitted in a low tone as he slipped an arm under her knees and swept her off her feet.

Lauren felt faint with desire. And not simply because it had been forever since she'd had sex;

since she'd felt loved and cherished. The need to feel a man's arms around her, to feel him buried deep inside her, had lain dormant for so long she'd almost forgotten what it felt like—until the incredibly sexy Caleb Hunter appeared on her doorstep and sent her libido into a tailspin.

"You okay?" he whispered, gazing down at her with concern. "Feels like I lost you."

"Sorry. I'm fine, please continue."

He chuckled, a sexy masculine rumble. "Yes, ma'am."

She tunneled her fingers through his hair as he spun them around and carefully laid her on the bed. He stretched out beside her, his head propped on one hand while the other moved over her body in almost worshipful fashion, tracing the curves of her breasts, the flare of her hip, the smooth line of her legs. He gently stroked his way back up, past the apex of her thighs, brushing against the golden curls— making her breath catch—before leaning in to dip his tongue into her navel.

Lauren clutched the bedspread beneath her in a death grip to keep from catapulting off the bed. Every inch of her hummed with anticipation as he slipped his fingers beneath the waistband of her thong and slowly peeled the tiny scrap of material down her legs. She lifted her feet so he could remove them, expecting him to slip her stilettos off as well. He didn't. Instead, he climbed off the bed and stood before her as he grasped the button of his jeans.

Lauren watched with feminine appreciation as he unbuttoned his jeans and slid the zipper down, slowly, as if giving her one last chance to back out. But thoughts of fleeing had long since dissipated, and all she longed to do was strip those jeans off him herself and have her way with him.

A shameless floozy only in her own mind, however, she settled for merely ogling him as he worked the well-worn denim down his muscular thighs and legs. He dropped them to the floor and kicked them aside. The proof of his desire swelled unmistakably behind his boxer-briefs.

A slow throb flared to life in her lower belly as he yanked them off and freed his hard length. Her heart thudded crazily as she took in his powerfully built arms and shoulders, his broad chest, lean abs, and those thickly muscled thighs. He truly was the most amazing man she'd ever laid eyes on.

Caleb lay down beside her, gathering her in his arms again and molding his hard frame against her soft curves. He stroked a hand down her back as he reclaimed her mouth. His hot tongue plunged between her lips, exploring, searching, demanding yet coaxing.

Lauren twined her arms around his neck and opened to him completely—her mouth and her body. She hooked one thigh over his and met the thrust of his tongue with equal fervor. Caleb held her so tight it was a miracle she didn't snap in two. His spicy masculine scent invaded her senses, wafting around her like a heady summer breeze, full of promise and scorching heat.

He broke the kiss and rolled her onto her back, his eyes full of promise as he leaned down to kiss her cheek, trailing a searing path along her jaw, down her throat, nipping at her shoulder before continuing onward. He slid one hand beneath her and palmed her butt, squeezing gently, drawing a ragged groan from deep in her chest.

Oh, God, she was so wet, so ready for him. But Caleb wasn't through playing, and he positioned himself over her, stroking a flaming path from her backside, over her thighs and belly until his warm palm settled over her aching breast. Desperate to feel his hot mouth on her tender nipple, she silently urged him on, threading her fingers though his hair, arching into him with a soft moan.

Thankfully, Caleb needed no further coaxing. He leaned in and tongued her nipple, sucking the sensitive pink flesh into his wet mouth, dragging his teeth over the pebbled tip, then blowing softly as if to soothe the pain. After paying homage to both breasts, he looked up, and the intensity in those mesmerizing brown pools nearly stole her breath. On instinct, she let her thighs fall apart, and that was all the invitation necessary. Caleb smoothed his hand over the flat plane of her stomach, through the golden thatch of curls at the apex of her thighs, until his fingers found her swollen pearl.

With a soft purr, Lauren arched into his hands, spreading her legs for him, giving him full access to her body. He captured her lips again, devouring her mouth with masterful thoroughness, as his fingers circled and stroked, rubbed and caressed, driving her to the brink of explosion. She gasped into his mouth when he finally sank two fingers inside her.

She tore her mouth free, her breath coming out in ragged pants. "Caleb, I'm…I'm so close…too close..."

"Let it happen, sweetheart," he whispered back, his voice ragged. "Let me pleasure you. God, you're so damn beautiful."

As she blossomed under his masterful touch, Lauren felt beautiful. She cupped his five o'clock shadow-roughened face with both hands and pulled him to her, needing to feel his lips on hers as he drove her to the gates of insanity.

Lauren loved to kiss, and Caleb certainly didn't disappoint. He slanted his mouth across hers, the rhythm of his tongue matching his magical fingers, stroke for delicious stroke.

Feverish with need, her skin grew taught as every pleasure point in her body throbbed for release. Her hips moved, rising up to meet his sexual onslaught. He suddenly broke the kiss and crouched down to draw one of her nipples into his hot mouth. He suckled it, hard, and that was all it took for Lauren to reach climax. She cried out, digging her heels into the mattress as she moved her hips in frantic rhythm with his fingers. Once the last tremor rolled through her, she collapsed into the mattress with a lusty sigh. Slightly embarrassed by her enthusiastic display, a self-conscious laugh quickly followed.

Her laughter turned into a squawk as Caleb flipped them over and settled her astride his hips, his steely erection nestled snuggly against her backside. He grinned with masculine satisfaction. "Liked that, did you?"

Chapter Ten

Lauren propped her hands on his chest and gave a one-shoulder shrug. "Eh. It was all right."

Laughter rumbled in his chest. "Damn, darlin', I thought you were going to bring the roof down on us."

Her cheeks flamed, but that sassy spirit he'd come to love shined through when she tweaked his chest hair.

Love? Ah, shit… Could it be? After all these years of managing to avoid a single attachment, had he fallen in love in just a matter of days? Was that even possible? He couldn't remember the last time he'd wanted a woman this much…maybe never. His need for her was a little overwhelming, to say the least. He'd lusted after his fair share of women, sure, but lust had never felt like this before. And he hadn't even made love to her yet.

Damn, there's that L word again.

Wiping all thoughts from his mind but one, Caleb reached up and cupped her breasts, caressing her soft, supple skin, teasing her nipples with his thumbs, watching the succulent pink tips tighten into needy buds. Having gotten over her initial nerves, Lauren arched into his hands with a hearty moan and wiggled her sweet ass against his straining erection.

He gave her nipples a playful pinch. "Careful. As turned on as I am, I've got about five minutes for you, tops."

Lauren laughed, and his gaze centered on her delectable mouth. He gripped her hips to hold her still. She leaned forward to rest her elbows on his chest and nip at his chin, lifting up to free him so that his sex was now sandwiched between them. "That long? Oh, I think I can get you there faster than that."

"Someone's awfully cocky," he drawled, sliding his hands down to her shapely backside. He squeezed, eliciting a sexy little gasp from her, then kissed her hard, bringing one hand up to palm the back of her head and hold her steady while he plundered her mouth.

As their lips and tongues mated, Lauren shifted to the side and wrapped her fingers around his erection. She caressed his hard shaft, learning every inch of him with gentle strokes. Caleb traced a hand down the silky flesh of her belly, loving the way she shivered at his touch. He found the swollen nub between her plump folds again and reveled in her sexy gasp as he caressed her, wanting her to climax again while he was deep inside her.

She pulled back and held his gaze, all traces of humor gone from her eyes. "Make love to me, Caleb. I want you…so much."

Christ, he couldn't speak, couldn't think. All he knew was this powerful need to love this beautiful woman. "Condoms?" he managed to choke out.

"Left-hand coat pocket," she purred against his throat.

He leaned over, snatched up the coat, and quickly dug the condoms from the pocket. All four of them. Seemed as if Carrie was good to babysit for quite a while. Thank you, Carrie. He tossed three onto the nightstand, and quickly tore the fourth open.

Quickly sheathing himself, Caleb rolled over and pulled Lauren into his arms, claiming her lips, desperate to bury himself between her thighs. She kissed him hungrily, hooking her left leg over his hip as she curled her fingers around his throbbing shaft and guided him to her welcoming heat. Caleb needed no further coaxing. He positioned himself at the opening of her body and slid into heaven. They came together hard and fast, their bodies growing slick with perspiration as they strained together. Lauren wrapped her legs around his hips, her heels digging into his ass as she met him thrust for thrust, those sexy gasps mingling with his guttural moans of pleasure.

Wrapped in her velvety softness, a flood of emotion suddenly seized him. Caleb buried his face in the crook of her neck and moved inside her with long, deep thrusts. He wanted, more than anything, to please this incredible woman, to completely rock her world.

Lauren clutched his back as she rose up to meet him, whispering barely intelligible words of encouragement as Caleb drove inside her with hard, swift strokes. She cried out, her inner walls clenching around him, her fingernails raking his back as she gyrated against him. Lauren's climax triggered his own release, and Caleb came with a raw, drawn out groan.

Once their bodies cooled and their breathing slowed, Caleb rolled to his side and pressed his lips to her temple. She snuggled deeper in his embrace and sighed. A very contented whisper of sound.

Caleb grew pensive as a fresh wave of confusing emotions washed over him. He adored this woman; his attraction to her was undeniable, beyond compare. He'd also grown quite fond of her kids and had started to bond with both of them. But Christ, that brought him right back to his earlier misgivings. They'd only known each other such a short time. And though his heart was urging him to stick around and take a chance, his head reminded him of just how disastrous this could be if things didn't work out.

Lauren pressed her hand against his chest, right over his heart, and Caleb heaved a silent, heartfelt sigh. Whatever his decision, he'd have to make it soon. Because the last thing he wanted to do was leave three broken hearts behind if he ultimately decided to head back to Chicago.

Or would that be four broken hearts?

"Wow, it's even busier than last year," Lauren announced as they strolled along the bustling fairway the following evening. Game operators beckoned them forward with promises of giant stuffed toys and other prizes. Screams and laughter could be heard from all around as people enjoyed the many rides and attractions the fair offered. The air was ripe with the aromas of every kind of food imaginable, from brats and deep-fried cheese curds, to elephant ears and candy apples. And Lauren's personal favorite—fresh, buttery caramel corn.

"Yep, sure is packed," Caleb said, sounding oddly disinterested. He'd seemed preoccupied from the moment he'd arrived at her house. Well, if she were being honest, he'd seemed preoccupied as he'd walked her to her car last night after several hours of lovemaking. Lauren had blamed his less than enthusiastic send-off on the late hour and physical exhaustion, but now she wasn't so sure as doubts started to creep into her head.

"Momma, cot' candy, cot' candy!" Emma insisted, bouncing in her stroller as they passed a vendor selling the fluffy, sugary clouds.

"Which color do you want, punkin?" Caleb asked as he pulled his wallet out.

She pointed to pink, and squealed when Caleb handed her the sweet treat.

"Thank you," Lauren said, trying not to worry over his distant attitude.

"Like I said, the day's on me."

His smile seemed genuine, and Lauren took heart. Maybe the fair reminded him of his mother, she thought as they continued down the fairway.

She had just placed Emma on a kiddie ride of slowly spinning airplanes when Max showed up, his arms full of carnival loot.

"Look at all the stuff I won!" he exclaimed, beaming, happier than she'd seen him in months.

Lauren's heart swelled with relief as she approached him to surreptitiously sniff for cigarette smoke. All she smelled was the caramel corn he had clutched in his hand. Max loved the stuff almost as much as she did. He rolled his eyes when she reached in for a handful.

"Here, you can have the rest if I can have a funnel cake."

Lauren grinned. "Deal." She accepted the small paper bag. "Why don't you run your stuff home before your arms fall off? I'll buy you that funnel cake when you get back."

"Cool."

Lauren watched him the entire way until he stuck his key in the back door. Living directly behind the fairgrounds was a blessing in

Lauren's eyes, although at night it could be an annoyance, especially when she wanted to get Emma to sleep.

Once the ride came to a stop, Caleb plucked Emma from the tiny airplane and lifted her up on his shoulders. Lauren smiled up at them. What a truly heartening picture they made. Except when she met Caleb's gaze, he cleared his throat and looked away. Lauren was almost sure she saw uncertainty in his eyes. Or was that...regret?

"How 'bout we get something to eat when Max gets back?" he suggested.

"I'cream, I'cream!" Emma demanded, bouncing on his shoulders.

Caleb chuckled as he set her back in her stroller and buckled her in.

Max came running up, panting. "Okay." More panting. "Ready for my funnel cake."

Lauren laughed. Caleb cocked a brow and she explained, "Last year, Max waited until the last minute to buy one. They ran out of batter and closed the stand before we got there."

Caleb clapped Max on the back. "Well, we can't let history repeat itself, so let's go. My treat."

"Cool!"

"And I'll split an ice cream cone with Emma." Lauren wheeled the stroller around and the four of them walked back toward the line of concession stands.

Lauren got in line at the custard stand and smiled with pleasure when she recognized Tara Russell walking down the fairway with Sugar, her brother Charlie's Great Dane. "Tara, over here!" Lauren flapped her arms to get her friend's attention.

Tara heard her, but searched around for a second before spotting them. She steered Sugar their way, and Lauren couldn't help but laugh as the dog snorted up crumbs the entire way.

"Hey, Lauren, I've been meaning to stop in for a trim."

Lauren let out a wistful sigh. All that beautiful silky black hair and Tara wouldn't let her play with it. "Someday you're going to let me do more than just take a half inch off the ends." With a raised brow, she took in Tara's odd choice in clothing and her multitude of tattoos. Daisy Dukes and a chain wrapped around her waist? "You guys celebrating Halloween in July this year?"

"What?"

Lauren grinned. "Between the Haunted House I saw on the way in and your costume, I don't know what else to think."

"Ha, ha, funny. I'm working the tattoo booth later."

"Ah, well, that makes more sense."

Tara rolled her eyes, and then smiled down at Emma. "Hey, Emma, is Mommy getting you some ice cream?"

"We share it," Emma explained, holding up a bandaged hand. "Owie."

"I see that." Tara glanced at Lauren. "What happened? Is she okay?"

"Yeah, she's fine. She burned her fingers on a lit cigarette. Some punk friend of Max's flicked it into the backyard, and Emma grabbed it before Max could stop her." The thought of what happened still caused Lauren's pulse to quicken. She accepted the large twist cone from the man behind the counter and handed him two singles.

"Poor little girl." Tara met Lauren's gaze, her eyes brimming with genuine concern. "And how awful for you, too."

"Not being able to take her pain away was the worst part. I was such a wreck. I don't know what I would've done if Caleb hadn't been there."

Tara raised a brow. "Caleb?"

Before Lauren could reply, Emma cried, "Momma, I'cream, I'cream!"

She knelt down and helped Emma grasp the cone with her unbandaged hand. "Careful, honey. Don't drop it." Lauren stood back up and pointed to where Max and Caleb were waiting in line for funnel cakes. "Caleb."

Tara looked him up and down. "Where have you been hiding him? I didn't know you were dating anyone." Tara's attention suddenly shot to Sugar, and Lauren realized with a start that Emma was about to share their ice cream with her.

"Oh, no, honey, don't do that!" Tara exclaimed. "She can't have—" Sugar wolfed down the ice cream cone so fast Lauren never had time to react.

Emma's eyes grew round and red with tears. Her lower lip trembled, and Lauren braced herself for the storm. Sugar hadn't touched Emma's hand, so Lauren knew her cries were simply over the loss of her treat.

"Sugar," Tara scolded, giving the dog's leash a hard tug, yanking her back a few steps. She met Lauren's gaze. "I'm sorry."

Lauren smiled reassuringly, then crouched down and ruffled Emma's hair. "It's okay, baby, I'll get us another one."

"Let me get it," Tara offered.

"Sassy doggie," Emma pouted, scowling at Sugar.

"Really, Tara, it's no big deal." Lauren was hard pressed not to laugh as Sugar licked her chops, tail thumping the ground, no doubt ready for another treat.

Tara tossed some money to the guy at the custard stand. "Actually, Charlie will pay me back, so I insist." She leaned down toward Emma. "Sorry about that, sweetie. We'll go now so she doesn't try to steal the next one. I'll see you later for that trim, Lauren—and the full scoop on that one." She grinned, indicating Caleb with a jerk of her head. Lauren and Emma both waved as Tara led Sugar away.

The vendor handed Lauren a second cone just as Caleb and Max approached, munching away on their funnel cakes.

"What happened?" Max asked. "We heard Emma crying, but all I saw was Tara and Sugar."

"Emma decided to share our ice cream with Sugar, who wasn't in the mood to share." Lauren handed Emma the replacement cone, and then gestured toward their funnel cakes. "How are they?"

Caleb held his out to her. "Awesome, try a bite."

"Don't mind if I do." *He seems back to his normally cheerful self,* she thought as she leaned in for a nibble. "Mmm, delicious."

Max chowed his down, then licked his fingers clean of powdered sugar. "I'm still hungry. Can I go get an ice cream cone, too?"

Lauren reached into her purse, but Caleb stopped her. "Put your money away. Like I said, the day's on me." He handed Max a five and grinned when the kid snatched it out of his hand and took off like a rocket.

"You're welcome!" Lauren shouted after him, exasperated by his lack of manners. "Sorry," she said to Caleb.

He waved it off. "He's just excited. This is probably the first time in a year he's let himself have fun. The kid's too hard on himself."

"Just wait until I ground him for the smoking. I swear he won't see the outside of his room for two weeks."

Caleb took another bite of his funnel cake and looked off into the distance. "I realize I don't have a say in the matter, but I truly believe you might be better off just letting it go. He's not going to smoke anymore, he promised."

Spoken like someone who doesn't have kids. Lauren let out a sigh. "Look, I realize you don't have any parenting experience, but you can't honestly believe Max shouldn't be punished just because he promised to never do it again. What else was he going to say?"

"I get it. I'm not his father and therefore shouldn't have an opinion."

"That's not what I meant, I—"

Caleb held up a hand, his expression rueful. "Christ, I'm sorry. Listen to me, acting as if I should have some say in how you discipline your kids."

"Caleb, you're the first person to ever show an interest in Max, and I appreciate your input more than I can say. It's just...after I found out what Max and his friends had been up to, all I could think was, 'My ten-year-old little boy's been smoking?'"

"Liar!" Max shouted from behind them. "You swore you wouldn't tell!"

Chapter Eleven

$\mathcal{L}$auren and Caleb both swung around at Max's outraged accusation.

"Honey, it's not what you think," Lauren tried to assure him, hating the thought of losing all of the progress he and Caleb had made. Why couldn't she have just kept her mouth shut and let the subject drop, at least for tonight?

Caleb clasped Max's shoulder. "I'm sorry, buddy. I didn't mean for this to happen."

Max twisted away from him, his eyes brimming with hurt and anger. "I trusted you!" Before either of them could respond, Max whipped his cone into the dirt and took off running.

"Max!" Lauren yelled. She started after him, but Caleb caught her by the arm.

"I'll go find him. I don't want you trying to handle him in his present frame of mind. He needs to get his anger out and cool down before he's ready to listen, and I'd rather I be his punching bag than you. Please," he added when she opened her mouth to argue.

Lauren gave a reluctant nod, feeling as if her stomach had just dropped to her feet. She watched Caleb give chase and wished she'd simply listened to the man instead of assuming she knew best where Max was concerned. Okay, yeah, nobody knew her son better than she did. But he was getting older, crossing the threshold from little boy into young man, and mothers weren't exactly welcomed over that threshold. Max was at an age where he couldn't even conceive she'd be able to relate to anything going on in his head.

Not that she could. And she hated that she may very well have pushed Max back into his self-destructive ways.

Twenty minutes went by with no appearance by Max or Caleb. Lauren was about to push a very sleepy Emma home when someone called her name. She glanced around until her gaze landed on Tara's brother, Charlie. He strode toward her, that killer smile in place. Lauren adored Charlie. In fact, she secretly thought of him as a big brother.

"Hey, beautiful, having a good time?" He walked up and draped an arm around her shoulder.

"Not exactly," she murmured, leaning slightly into him.

"What's wrong? Any chance I can help?"

Lauren smiled up at him, praying her eyes didn't betray her inner turmoil. Last thing she wanted to do was burden Charlie with this, and she wasn't exactly anxious to tell anyone about Max and the smoking. "Thanks, but no. Just girl stuff. I have cramps." She added the latter with a teasing grin.

With an uncomfortable chuckle, Charlie stepped back and turned to face her. "Listen, I was wondering, would you want to catch a movie sometime, or maybe go out to dinner?"

Lauren gaped at him in stunned silence. Was Charlie asking her out on a date?

"I, uh—"

Two very possessive arms snaked around her, trapping her against a warm, broad chest. "Yeah, I don't see that happening," Caleb said. He tipped her chin up and kissed her, and while his display of jealousy was flattering, she couldn't help feeling bad for Charlie, who looked surprisingly angry.

She tore free of Caleb's arms and frowned at him before turning to face Charlie. "I'm really sorry—"

Charlie held up a hand and spared her, the smile on his face not quite reaching his eyes. "No, I'm sorry. I didn't realize you were seeing someone." He dropped the smile and met Caleb's steely gaze in silent warning, then turned and strode away.

Lauren pushed her frustration aside and turned back to Caleb. "Did you find Max?"

Caleb propped his hands on his hips and gave his head a quick shake. "Sorry. I think we should head back to your place and check there. If he's not home, you can stay and put Emma to bed, and I'll run back out to find him."

"Fine. Let's go."

Lauren wheeled Emma's stroller around to head home when someone ran by and hollered, "Hey, there's a kid hanging from the top of the Ferris wheel! Someone call the fire department!"

Lauren froze as a bad feeling settled in her chest.

"My God, it can't be..."

They both swung around, and Lauren cried out when she spotted her son, legs swinging, arms wrapped around a crossbar as he hung on for dear life.

"Holy shit!" Caleb raced off, and with a sob, Lauren took off after him, struggling to push

Emma's stroller across the rock and garbage-strewn dirt fairway. Caleb was talking furiously with the ride operator when Lauren reached his side.

"Max, hold on, baby! Please, just hold on tight! We're going to have you down from there in no time, I promise! No, don't look down!" she added in a near screech.

Caleb ran over to her. "I'm climbing up there myself. We don't have time to wait for the fire truck, and if the operator tries to bring the car down, it's doubtful Max could hang on with all the jerking."

"Please," she choked out, frightened out of her mind. "Save my son."

Caleb met her terrified gaze and gave a curt nod. No way in hell would he do anything less.

He cupped a hand over his eyes and studied the structure of the ride for a nanosecond, trying to figure out the best route to the top. He gave an apologetic grimace to the frightened couple in the bottom car before pulling himself up on top of it. Nimbly, Caleb climbed one bar at a time. The chaos below him faded to white noise as he continued to climb, his sole focus on the boy who'd grown to mean more to him in just six days than he ever could've imagined.

Too damn bad it took a possible life and death situation for him to realize it.

When he was within five feet of touching Max's feet, he said, "Listen to me, Max. I'm going to get you down, but I need you to stay calm, okay? Hang on tight and do exactly as I tell you."

He could just make out Max's upper face, and his heart broke over the stark fear in the kid's eyes. Max was smart, though. He stared straight ahead without looking down. Caleb swallowed hard and reminded himself to focus. He'd never felt such immense terror before, not even when under enemy fire overseas.

He managed to maneuver himself directly beneath Max's dangling feet. "All right, listen carefully, Max. When I say so, I want you to slowly lower yourself until you're sitting on my shoulders. Once there, I can help you slide down until your arms and legs are wrapped around me piggyback-style. Got it?"

Max swallowed hard and gave a quick nod. "I-I'm sorry. I wanted to get off, but the stupid guy wouldn't bring me down. So I-I tried to climb down."

Jesus H. Christ. "We'll talk about how foolish that was later. What matters right now is getting you down from here safe and sound." Caleb steadied himself and made sure he had a secure hold on the thick metal spoke. He had one foot braced against the inner wheel, and his other leg wrapped around the same spoke he held in a death grip. When he felt he had as secure a hold as he could, he said, "Okay, Max, it's time. Do exactly as I told you to—and take your time."

Max was quiet as a church mouse as he tentatively lowered himself, one inch at a time. Caleb grasped his ankle to help guide him; Max panicked and let out a choked cry.

"It's okay, son. I'm not going to let you fall. Just keep on—" Gears ground a split second before the Ferris wheel jerked. Max screamed as his grip was torn loose and he fell. Cries and shrieks from the crowd below rose up as Caleb caught Max like a sack of potatoes only in reverse, as if Max had been sitting on his shoulders and fell backward.

"I got you, buddy, you aren't going anywhere. Just close your eyes and breathe. Hear that siren? The fire truck will be here any second."

Caleb could feel Max's heartbeat hammering against his back. Please God, give me the strength to hold on until the fire truck arrives.

And then it was there. The most welcome sight Caleb had ever seen. He watched as the fire truck steered into place, then several firemen climbed down and got to work.

In no time, an aerial ladder telescoped up to them, and Caleb helped get Max safely into the firefighter's arms. By the time Caleb was safely on the ground, a sobbing Lauren had Max crushed in her arms.

Caleb couldn't even put words to the emotions coursing through him. If he hadn't been sure before, he had no doubts now. He wanted Lauren, Max, and Emma in his life. And he planned to stay in Redemption permanently. This was his home—always had been in his heart, even if he'd been too angry for the past twenty years to admit it.

Lauren reluctantly let Max go to be checked for injuries, then rushed to Caleb's side. Her beautiful face gazed up at him, and all he could think about was how much he wanted to kiss her.

"You saved my son's life. I don't even know how to begin to pay you for that."

Caleb reached out and cupped her cheek. "I'm crazy about that boy. Emma, too."

"And they're crazy about you," she countered, her expression guarded.

He wondered if she was feeling as insecure and vulnerable as he was right now. "Good to know. But what about their mother? Any feelings of adoration there?"

The most incredible smile spread across her face as she gazed up at him with her heart in her eyes. "I happen to know firsthand their mother's adoration for you is only exceeded by her desire to kiss you."

He slipped his arm around her and pulled her close, but before they could give in to "her desire," Max approached, feet dragging in the dirt. Caleb gave her a quick squeeze, stepped back, and waited for Max to speak.

"Am I grounded?"

Caleb couldn't help but chuckle. Lauren was less amused. She crossed her arms and said, "I think you know the answer to that. And just for the record, Caleb didn't rat you out, one of the neighbors did. So not only are you grounded for two weeks, but you owe this very brave man a thank you and an apology."

Max cast Caleb a quick glance. "I'm sorry," he mumbled. "I didn't wanna believe you narced me out, but that's what it sounded like."

"I know." Caleb clapped him on the back. "Apology accepted."

Lauren glanced up at the darkening sky. The sun had nearly finished its descent into the western horizon and would be completely gone in a matter of minutes. "Why don't we head over to the field and find a spot to watch the fireworks?" She crouched down and peeked at Emma, who'd managed to snore right through all the excitement. The love that shone from her eyes as she gazed upon her daughter made Caleb's chest ache in an unfamiliar yet very welcome way.

They hustled down to the baseball field, spread out the blanket Lauren had remembered to tuck into Emma's stroller, and settled in to watch the display. Emma finally roused and insisted on sitting in Max's lap. Caleb sat with one knee up and one hand propped behind him, Lauren leaning against his shoulder.

The oddest sense of peace washed over him as the first burst of color exploded in the sky. As Max and Emma "oohed" and "ahhed," Caleb leaned down and kissed Lauren, sealing their fate under a blazing canopy of red, white, and blue.

Author's Note

I hope you enjoyed Lauren and Caleb's story. Max and Emma are close to my heart as my they were my mother's favorite characters. Stacey Joy Netzel and I would love for you to read the rest of the series and fall in love with the characters who've become our friends.

— *Donna Marie Rogers*

Thank you for reading!

If you enjoyed *A Fair of the Heart*, don't forget to leave a review.

Visit Donna's website to sign up for her newsletter for announcements of all New Releases and *exclusive* sales and content!

www.DonnaMarieRogers.com

Up next in the WELCOME TO REDEMPTION series

A Fair to Remember

Welcome to Redemption Series
Book 2

STACEY JOY NETZEL

Reformed gang member Wes Carter feels Redemption, Wisconsin, is just the place to relocate his financial business for reasons more than just the name. He's ready for a nice, quiet life in small town USA. Tara Russell has decided it's time to add some excitement to her life and get a little wild—no matter how uncomfortable it makes her or her overprotective family. They meet at the local fair one warm summer night and discover opposites attract for all the right reasons. Add a dash of Sugar in the form of an incorrigible Great Dane, and it's destined to be *A Fair To Remember*.

Excerpt

$\mathcal{W}$es Carter took another bite of his hamburger and surveyed the baseball diamond in front of him as he savored the flavor of his cheap burger with ketchup and mustard. If the number of men on the far side of the field were any indication, they were planning quite the pyrotechnics display for later tonight. He might just have to hang around for that, he hadn't watched fireworks in years.

He'd had a feeling about this town when he'd read the business listings on the Internet—and not only because of the name. Further research revealed Redemption to be just what he was looking for.

Well, except for the stalker with the dog.

A wry grin lifted his lips as he scanned the immediate area. It looked like he'd finally lost her. During the few glances he'd snuck, he'd noticed her trim figure in shorts and sexy tank, with just the right amount of curves up top, and a bouncing ponytail of shiny black hair that would reach all the way down her back when set free. He loved long hair.

But whoa, he was getting off track. Between the bikers he'd seen her chumming with, and the tatts on her arms, she appeared to walk farther on the wild side than he was comfortable with these days. Hell, she even had one on her neck...her slim, delicate, tanned neck. *Wild*. Maybe crazy was more like it the way she'd followed him around with that hulking monster of a dog.

Wild and crazy, and pretty to boot...he felt a little zing nip at his pulse. Yeah, he was the crazy one now. He was done with women like that, and, yes, he knew all about them, he'd grown up with them. A twinge of pain in his back made him wince, despite the fact the sensation remained only in his head. Though the wound had healed weeks ago, it kept reminding him of all he'd left behind—the big city fast track with the crime and the gangs.

No more looking over his shoulder, and wild women didn't fit into the nice, quiet, stable life he planned to build in this town. No matter how pretty they were.

"Sugar! Heel!"

Wes started to look over his shoulder at the sound of that sharp command called out so close behind him, but he never made it past the pitching mound. Next thing he knew, he laid face first in the grass, his hamburger smashed against his chest and a heavy weight on his back. He turned his head to the side so he could breath and something wet and warm doused his face from chin to eyebrow.

"Ugh," he managed, concluding pretty quick that a dog stood on his back—a large, whining, panting monster of a dog. He hunched a shoulder and wiped the slobber as best he could, but the beast did it again.

"Oh, God, I'm sorry."

He twisted his head to look in the direction of the voice. Slim ankles and tanned legs registered before that side of his face got swiped. That's it—he preferred to eat dirt.

"I'm so sorry," the woman continued, "she just pulled right—"

"Get it off me," he said into the grass.

"What? I'm sorry, I didn't—"

Wes turned his head with a frustrated growl, which only excited the dog into a licking frenzy. Its massive paws dug into his shoulder blades as Wes clenched his teeth to keep its tongue out of his mouth.

"Get. It. Off."

"Oh, right, sorry." He felt her tug on the leash. "Sugar, *heel*."

He mentally rolled his eyes. Obviously, that was a useless command.

"Sugar, come on. Here, baby. Sugar."

The dog went still and made a sound deep in its throat. Wes frowned when the animal did it again. That's when it dawned on him the woman's pleas had become urgent.

"No, Sugar. Off. Sugar! Come!"

That didn't sound good. He fought to free his arms from under his body and succeeded just as the brute made a horrible retching noise and something spilled onto his back—something very liquid-y and warm that spread even as it seeped through his clothes.

"Sugarrrrrr," the woman groaned.

Silence fell except for the dog's panting.

Wes felt his own stomach rebel. "Tell me a dog didn't just puke on my back."

A Fair To Remember is available now at your favorite bookstore or online retailer.

About the Author

USA Today Bestselling author Donna Marie Rogers inherited her love of romance from her mother. Romance novels, soap operas, *Little House on the Prairie*—her mother loved them all. And though it wasn't until years later Donna would come to understand her mother's fascination with Charles Ingalls, Donna's love of the romance genre is every bit as all-consuming.

A Chicago native, Donna now lives in beautiful Northeast Wisconsin with her husband and children. She's an avid gardener and home-canner, as well as an admitted Halloween fanatic. Her passion to read is only exceeded by her passion to write, so when she's not doing the wife and mother thing, you can usually find her sitting at the computer, creating exciting, memorable characters, fresh new worlds, and always happily-ever-afters.

www.DonnaMarieRogers.com

www.ingramcontent.com/pod-product-compliance
Lightning Source LLC
Chambersburg PA
CBHW050946120626
46552CB00001B/401

* 9 7 8 1 9 4 1 8 2 9 0 7 3 *